A Friend Named Crapface . . .

Clint didn't know where the little buffalo hunter was, but he knew wherever he was, he was looking down the barrel of his .50-caliber rifle. He knew Crapface had his back.

The other ranch hands all had sweating palms, and as Gary Vernon wiped his dry on his trousers, they did the same thing. Their orders were to watch Lukas and move when he moved. Their target was the Gunsmith, but they were all wondering where the smelly buffalo hunter with the Big Fifty was.

A bullet from that gun could tear a man in half.

Clint watched Lukas's face and knew that, no matter what happened, the man was going to draw. No question about it. He was that stupid. The only question was how stupid the other five were.

Just then he heard it.

Crapface had just cocked the hammer on the Big Fifty. That wasn't a sound you could mistake. And the street was quiet enough for it to carry.

"Okay, ranch hand," Clint said to Lukas. "Let's see how many of your friends we can get killed."

THE GUNSMITH

365

THE LAST BUFFALO HUNT

J. R. ROBERTS

JOVE BOOKS, NEW YORK

THE BERKLEY PUBLISHING GROUP
Published by the Penguin Group
Penguin Group (USA) Inc.
375 Hudson Street, New York, New York 10014, USA
Penguin Group (Canada), 90 Eglinton Avenue East, Suite 700, Toronto, Ontario M4P 2Y3, Canada
(a division of Pearson Penguin Canada Inc.) • Penguin Books Ltd., 80 Strand, London WC2R 0RL,
England • Penguin Group Ireland, 25 St. Stephen's Green, Dublin 2, Ireland (a division of Penguin
Books Ltd.) • Penguin Group (Australia), 250 Camberwell Road, Camberwell, Victoria 3124, Australia
(a division of Pearson Australia Group Pty. Ltd.) • Penguin Books India Pvt. Ltd., 11 Community
Centre, Panchsheel Park, New Delhi—110 017, India • Penguin Group (NZ), 67 Apollo Drive,
Rosedale, Auckland 0632, New Zealand (a division of Pearson New Zealand Ltd.) • Penguin Books
(South Africa) (Pty.) Ltd., 24 Sturdee Avenue, Rosebank, Johannesburg 2196, South Africa

Penguin Books Ltd., Registered Offices: 80 Strand, London WC2R 0RL, England

This is a work of fiction. Names, characters, places, and incidents either are the product of the author's imagination or are used fictitiously, and any resemblance to actual persons, living or dead, business establishments, events, or locales is entirely coincidental.

THE LAST BUFFALO HUNT

A Jove Book / published by arrangement with the author

PRINTING HISTORY
Jove edition / May 2012

Copyright © 2012 by Robert J. Randisi.
Cover illustration by Sergio Giovine.

ISBN: 978-0-515-15069-8

JOVE®
Jove Books are published by The Berkley Publishing Group,
a division of Penguin Group (USA) Inc.,
375 Hudson Street, New York, New York 10014.
JOVE® is a registered trademark of Penguin Group (USA) Inc.
The "J" design is a trademark of Penguin Group (USA) Inc.

PRINTED IN THE UNITED STATES OF AMERICA

10 9 8 7 6 5 4 3 2 1

ONE

Clint Adams wondered how many times he had gotten into trouble while minding his own business. And how many times it had happened when he stuck his nose where it didn't belong. If he had to bet, he would say it was fifty-fifty. Because it didn't seem to matter what he did—trouble either followed him, or was waiting for him.

He was in a small saloon in a small town in Nebraska—the town of Walton—working on a large mug of cold beer. The saloon was less than half full, and he had managed to get a table in the back. He was sitting with his back to the wall, and at the moment no one was paying any attention to him, which suited him just fine.

Then half a dozen men entered together, and suddenly the atmosphere went from sleepy to rowdy. The men gathered at the bar, ordered beer and whiskey, and proceeded to get drunk and even rowdier.

From watching and listening, Clint determined that

they were from a nearby ranch. The others in the saloon seemed to know them, and were steering clear of them. So for about half an hour their aggression was confined to the six of them.

When Clint ordered another beer from the one tired-looking saloon girl, he asked, "Who are those men?"

"Oh, them?" she said. "They're from the Crooked W. They're always comin' to town and causin' trouble. I was you, I'd stay away from them."

"I'm not looking to mix in with anybody here," he said. "Another quiet beer will do me fine."

"Comin' up."

She went to the bar and had to run a gauntlet of grabbing hands from the six cowboys. They all watched her walk back to Clint's table and set a beer down on it.

"You put up with that whenever they come to town?" he asked.

"All the time," she said. "They won't hurt a girl, but I've seen them do a lot of damage to men, and for no reason."

"What about the sheriff?"

"They beat him to within an inch of his life one day," she said. "He ain't been the same since."

She took his empty mug and walked away.

Two of the six men were still looking over at him, but when someone slapped them on the back, they turned away.

"Who you figure that feller in the corner is?" Tom Holliver asked.

Sam Walden looked over and said, "Dunno. Why do you care?"

"He's a stranger," Holliver said.

"So what?" Vic Miller asked. "Lots of strangers come to town."

"Yeah," Holliver said, "but they're the ones we usually have some fun with."

Dan Lukas said without looking up from his drink, "That feller don't look to me like the kind to have fun with."

Gary Vernon slapped Holliver on the back and said, "Dan's got a point, Tom. You better just turn around and finish your beer."

"Yeah," the sixth man, Hank Dennis, said, "they're right. 'Sides, somebody else'll come walkin' in soon. Somebody we can have lots of fun with."

"Yeah, I guess," Holliver said.

Tyrone Jones rode into the Nebraskan town of Walton and immediately attracted attention. He was used to that. Mostly, he presented the appearance of a pile of skins atop a horse. He was a small man, who wore a lot of buffalo skins. Most of his adult life had been spent hunting buffalo, and as the bison faded from the plains, so did Jones.

He reined in his horse in front of a small saloon and stepped down. He shrugged his skins into place comfortably, removed his Sharps Big Fifty from the saddle, then tied his horse off and entered the saloon.

As he passed between the batwing doors, the odor he projected had already preceded him. The other patrons all watched him as he headed for the bar. The six ranch hands already standing there turned and looked at him. They all had the same thought in mind.

Fun.

Jones reached the bar and knew what was coming. He

was used to being the butt of the joke. But that didn't mean that he ever took it lightly.

When Clint saw the man enter and approach the bar, he had one thought, and one thought only.

Crapface.

TWO

Crapface Jones didn't see Clint Adams sitting in the back of the room. He did see the faces of the six ranch hands at the bar, and knew what was coming.

"Beer," he told the bartender.

The man brought the beer and couldn't hide his reaction to the smell of Tyrone "Crapface" Jones's skins.

"Omigod!" Tom Holliver yelled. "Whoeeee! What is that smell?"

"I know what you mean," Vic Miller said, sniffing the air. "Where's that comin' from?"

"Jesus," Sam Walden said, "it's stinkin' up the whole room."

"Is there somethin' dead in here?" Gary Vernon asked, looking around.

Hank Dennis lifted his arms and sniffed his own armpits.

"It ain't me," he announced.

"Could be all of you," Dan Lukas said. "Fact of the matter is, it's this fella over here."

Holliver leaned toward Jones and sniffed.

"By God, he's right. This fella stinks. And his face looks like crap."

All the other men turned and looked.

"By God," Dennis said, "he's right. What the hell happened to your face, fella?"

The buffalo hunter ignored all of them and drank his beer.

"Hey," Sam Walden said, "we're talkin' to you."

Jones put his mug down and looked at them. They were all five-ten to just over six feet—easily half a foot taller than him.

"Look," he said, "I just came in here to have a beer. I ain't lookin' for no trouble."

"Well," Hank Dennis said, "you shoulda took a bath before you come in here stinkin' the place up."

"Yeah," Tolliver said. "Boys, I think maybe we better take this fella out to a horse trough and give him a good bath."

"That sounds like a good idea," Vic Miller said. "Whataya think, Dan?"

Now they all looked at Lukas, who was obviously the leader of the group.

"Get him out of here," he said. "He stinks. I don't care what you do with him outside."

"It's them skins," Dennis said.

"Naw, I think it's him," Tolliver said.

"Maybe it's those sores on his face," Gary Vernon said.

"Whatever it is," Lukas said, "get him outside."

Lukas remained with his elbows on the bar while the other five men moved toward the little buffalo hunter. Suddenly, the Sharps Big Fifty was in his hands and he looked a lot bigger.

"A bullet from this Big Fifty will tear a man in two," he said. "Who wants to be first?"

The five men froze. Dan Lukas turned his head and looked at Jones.

"He's only got one shot, and then he has to reload," Lukas said. "Go ahead and take him."

"But . . . he'll kill one of us, Dan," Tom Holliver said.

"Maybe," Lukas said. "That's a big gun, and this is close quarters. I'll bet you can jump him before he gets one of you."

"If you think they can do that, why don't you jump me?" Jones asked.

"Then I'd have to touch you," Lukas said. "I ain't about to touch you. No tellin' what kind of diseases you got inside them skins."

Jones didn't answer. He kept the Big Fifty steady. If they came at him, he was going to put a hole in somebody.

Dan Lukas turned and faced him.

"Okay," he said, "then we'll do it another way."

"How's that?" Jones asked.

"Six guns against one," Lukas said. "You might kill one of us but the rest of us will kill you. Unless . . ."

"Unless what?"

"You consent to take a bath."

"Where?"

"Outside," Lukas said, "in a horse trough. You put your gun down, my boys take you outside and give you a good dunkin'."

"And if I say no?"

"Like I said," Dan Lukas said, "six guns against one."

Jones looked at each of the six men in turn. A couple of them looked scared, the rest anxious. One thing he knew, they were all going to draw.

Before he could answer, though, a voice spoke from the back of the room.

"Make that two."

Dan Lukas turned and looked at the man who had spoken.

"What's that?"

"I said make that two," Clint said.

"Two what?" Lukas asked.

"Two guns," Clint said. "You said it was six guns against one. And I said, make it two. Six guns against two."

The other men looked at Clint.

Lukas said, "Do you know this man?"

"I do."

"This smelly little man?" Lukas asked, pointing at Jones. "You know him?"

"I said yes, I do."

"He, like, a friend of yours?"

"He is."

"So you know his name."

"I do. It's Jones."

"And you're willin' to step into this?" Lukas said. "For him?"

"That's right."

"Just to keep him from takin' a bath?"

"In a horse trough," Clint said. "He doesn't want to take a bath in a horse trough. Maybe, if you gave him a choice, he'd go and take a proper bath."

"But that ain't what I want," Lukas said.

"Well, maybe this isn't about what you want."

Lukas grinned.

"It's always about what I want, friend," Lukas said. "If you spend any more time in this town, you'll find that out."

"Well, I don't intend to spend much time in this pissant little town," Clint said. "Maybe just enough time to teach you six idiots a lesson."

Lukas looked at Jones, who hadn't moved, and then back at Clint.

"So you're serious about this."

"As a heart attack."

"What the hell is your name, friend?"

"Why does that matter?"

"I like to know who I'm killin'."

"Big talk for a ranch hand," Clint said.

"I'll show you what kind of ranch hand I am," Lukas said. He looked at Jones. "You know him?"

"Yeah."

"You know his name?"

"Sure I do."

"What is it?"

Jones looked at Clint.

"Should I tell 'im?"

Clint shrugged and said, "Go ahead."

"Yeah, go ahead," Lukas said. "Tell me who your friend is."

Jones looked at Dan Lukas and said, "His name's Clint Adams."

THREE

"That's bull crap!" Lukas said.

The saloon had gone totally silent.

"The Gunsmith?" Tom Holliver said.

"That's right," Jones said.

"I don't believe it," Lukas said.

"W-What if it is?" Hank Dennis said. "I mean, what if he is the Gunsmith?"

"So what?" Lukas asked. "What if he is the Gunsmith? There's still six of us and one of him."

"Two," Jones said. "Two against six."

"You?" Lukas said. "You can go, smelly man. Now it's just us and the Gunsmith."

"Naw," Jones said. "I'm stayin'."

"Dan—" Sam Walden said.

"Shut up, Sam!" Lukas said. "They're just tryin' to spook us."

"Doin' a good job on me," Hank Dennis said.

"Shut up!" Lukas said again. "Vic and Hank, you take the stink man. The rest of us will take the other fella."

"The Gunsmith?" Holliver asked.

"It don't matter who he is," Lukas insisted. "Whoever he is, he's gonna bleed when we shoot him."

"If you shoot me," Clint said.

They looked at him—except for the two men who were now watching Jones.

"You think you're fast enough to kill the four of us before one of us gets you?" Lukas demanded.

"Fast has got nothing to do with it," Clint said. "Look at your men."

Lukas looked.

"They're sweating," Clint said. "The palms of their hands are wet. They're going to rush their shots. I'm not."

Lukas seemed to be thinking things over.

"How bad do you want to give my friend a bath?" Clint asked.

Lukas looked at his men.

"Not bad enough to die over it," Holliver said.

The other men nodded.

"All right," Lukas said. "Okay. Back off." He looked at Clint. "You and your friend better get yerselves out of town."

"I don't know about my friend," Clint said, "but I'm leaving."

"Me, too," Jones said. "After one more beer."

"Yeah," Clint agreed, "one more beer."

Lukas abruptly headed for the door, and his men followed him. The last two men backed out, keeping their eyes on Clint and Jones.

When they were gone, Jones lowered his Big Fifty and looked at the bartender.

"Two beers," he said.

"Comin' up."

He put two beers on the table. Jones grabbed both mugs in one hand, held the Big Fifty in the other, and walked to Clint's table. The people around them leaned away, making faces. Some of them got up and left.

Jones put the beers down on the table, leaned his rifle against the wall, and then sat opposite Clint.

Clint pulled one of the beers over to him and said, "How are you, Crapface?"

"I guess I'm fine now," Jones said.

Calling him "Crapface" was no insult to the smaller man, because he had long ago decided that was his name. The scabs and pockmarks on his face had earned him that name from a young age. As he grew older, he accepted it.

"What are you doin' here?" he asked Clint.

"Just passing through," Clint said. "Thought I'd stop for a beer . . . or two." Then he raised his mug in his hand. "Or three."

"Three sounds good to me." Crapface took a long pull on his cold beer. "You think those fellas are gonna be waitin' outside for us?"

"Probably."

"Any more?"

"You got me," Clint said. "I only saw those six come in."

"Probably all there is," Jones said. "We could go out the back."

"We could."

"But you won't?"

"I can't afford to," Clint said.

"Oh, yeah," Crapface said, "that reputation of yours. Wouldn't want people to think you were scared."

"I can't afford that," Clint said.

"I know, I know," Crapface said. "Every two-bit gun hand would come out of the woodwork for a chance at you."

"That's right."

"Well," Jones said, "I suppose I could go out the back way."

"There's that."

Jones sat back.

"Let's catch up first," the buffalo hunter said. "What's been going on with you?"

"Same thing."

"Kill or be killed?"

"Sometimes."

"How would you like to do somethin' where you know nobody's tryin' to kill you?"

Clint studied the other man's face. Crapface's age had always been a mystery. At this point he knew the man had to be at least forty-five, but he could have been sixty-five or seventy.

"What do you have in mind?"

"A hunt."

Clint shook his head.

"There are no more buffalo."

Jones raised his index finger.

"One last hunt," he said.

"Where?"

"Texas panhandle."

"With who?"

"Me, a few others," Jones said.

"How many buffalo?"

"I'm not sure," Jones said. "I've heard different counts. Two hundred. Three hundred. Five hundred. I decided the only way for me to find out is to go there."

Clint thought about it. It had been years since he'd been on a real buffalo hunt. It was on a hunt years ago that he first met Bat Masterson and Wyatt Earp, the men who had become his most trusted friends.

"Are you headed there now?" Clint asked.

"I am."

Clint sipped his beer.

"Come with me," Jones said. "What have you got to lose?"

"Nothing."

"Exactly."

Jones extended his beer mug and Clint clinked it with his.

"Now we only have to get by those men outside," Jones said.

"They're still going to be nervous," Clint said.

"I'll go out the back, get up high," Jones said. "You gonna walk out into the street?"

Clint nodded.

"I'm glad I don't have your . . . rules."

"They're not rules," Clint said.

FOUR

When the six men got outside, Vic Miller said, "I sure would've liked to try that Gunsmith."

"We are."

"Huh?" Miller said.

"What?" Tom Holliver said.

"We're gonna wait out here for him," Lukas said, "and take him when he comes out."

"How the hell are we gonna do that?" Hank Dennis asked.

"Spread out," Lukas said. "Two of you to the right, two to the left. Find positions behind cover."

"We gonna bushwhack him?" Sam Walden asked.

"We're gonna bushwhack him, but make it look like we didn't bushwack him."

"And how do we do that?" Gary Vernon asked.

"You and me, Gary," Lukas said, "we're gonna stand in the street, make it look fair."

"In the street?" Vernon asked. "Me?"

"You *and* me," Lukas said.

Vernon looked at the other four men, who all looked away.

Jones left.

Clint waited ten minutes, letting the little buffalo hunter get set.

The people around him felt great relief as the smell began to dissipate.

Clint got up and walked to the front of the saloon. The other patrons all stayed where they were and watched him.

"How can you stand the smell?" the bartender asked him.

"You get used to it," Clint said. "Besides, I spent a lot of time around buffalo when I was younger."

Clint looked out the window.

"They'll be out there, ya know," the bartender said. "You made 'em look stupid."

"Bushwhackers?"

"Oh, yeah."

"What about the sheriff?"

"He won't be no help," the bartender said. "He'll come around when it's all over."

"Good to know."

"You goin' out?"

"Yes."

"And your friend?"

"He'll back my play."

"So two against six."

"Will it be only six?" Clint asked. "Or do they have more friends?"

"Are you really the Gunsmith?"

"Yes."

The barman shook his head.

"They won't get any other help," he said. "Just the six of them."

"Any of them any good with a gun?"

"Lukas thinks he is. He was the big mouth. But usually they just act as a gang."

"Okay," Clint said, "thanks for the help."

"Well," the bartender said, "ain't like I wanna get you mad at me."

"Don't worry about that," Clint said. "I reserve my anger for people who shoot at me."

"Good to know."

Clint walked to the batwing doors and stopped. From there he couldn't see anybody.

"Good luck," the bartender said.

FIVE

Clint stepped through the batwing doors.

"Took you long enough, Adams," Dan Lukas said.

The ranch hand was standing in the street with one other man. Either he couldn't get the other four to stand with him, or they were spread out behind cover. Clint voted for the latter. He doubted Lukas would be standing in the street with only one man to back him.

"Sorry if I kept you waiting," Clint said.

"You made me look like a fool in there," Lukas said. "In front of my friends."

"You pretty much made a fool of yourself," Clint said. "You didn't need any help. And I'm willing to bet you don't have any friends in there." He waved. "I'll bet all your friends are out here, hiding behind a barrel or in an alley."

"Whatsa matter?" Lukas said. "You don't like these odds? Two to one?"

"Cut the shit, Lukas," Clint said. "That's your name,

right? Lukas? If you're gonna make a move, make it. And you . . . get ready to draw or run."

Vernon swallowed hard.

"Wipe your palms on your pants," Clint told him.

Vernon did it.

"Don't listen to him, Gary," Lukas said.

Crapface Jones had managed to get himself up onto the roof of the saloon. From there he had clear sight of Clint Adams standing in the street facing two of the ranch hands. He didn't know their names, but that didn't matter much to him.

He sighted down the long barrel of his well-cared-for Big Fifty, scanned the street, and one by one picked out the locations of the other men. Eventually, he had all six of them spotted.

Now all he had to do was assign them numbers, so he knew who he was going to take first.

Clint didn't know where the little buffalo hunter was, but he knew wherever he was, he was looking down the barrel of his .50 caliber rifle. He knew Crapface had his back.

The other ranch hands all had sweating palms, and as Gary Vernon wiped his dry on his trousers, they did the same thing. Their orders were to watch Lukas and move when he moved. Their target was the Gunsmith, but they were all wondering where the smelly buffalo hunter with the Big Fifty was.

A bullet from that gun could tear a man in half.

Clint watched Lukas's face and knew that, no matter what happened, the man was going to draw. No question about it. He was that stupid. The only question was how stupid the other five were.

Just then he heard it.

Crapface had just cocked the hammer on the Big Fifty. That wasn't a sound you could mistake. And the street was quiet enough for it to carry.

"Okay, ranch hand," Clint said to Lukas. "Let's see how many of your friends we can get killed."

SIX

Dan Lukas drew.

Crapface blew a hole through Gary Vernon's chest. Pieces of Vernon flew all over the street.

Clint drew and fired one round into the chest of Dan Lukas. The ranch hand never got his gun out of his holster. He toppled over backward and hit the street with an audible thud.

The shots faded, and it got quiet again.

Clint and Crapface waited to see what the other four men were going to do. Clint knew his friend had reloaded, because once again he heard the hammer cock.

"The rest of you men come on out," Clint said. "Make your play or go back to your ranch."

Crapface had reloaded and watched as the four men stepped out from hiding. He assumed one of the dead men in the street was their leader. They stared down at him.

* * *

"Come closer," Clint said. "Take a good look. This is what stupidity got both of them. Now how stupid do you want to be?"

The four men stared down at the dead Lukas and blasted-apart Vernon.

"You men want to go for your guns?"

The four of them stared at him and Hank Dennis said, "No, sir."

"Then walk away, get on your horses, and leave town."

They turned to start walking away.

"Wait!"

They stopped.

"Leave your guns in the middle of the street."

The four men exchanged looks and then, one by one, they took their guns from their holsters and dropped them into the street.

"Now don't get brave with your rifles when you mount up," Clint told them.

"No, sir," Vic Miller said.

"Then get!"

They all looked up at the roof of the saloon, where Crapface was watching them over the barrel of his long gun.

Then they walked to their horses in front of the saloon, mounted up, and left.

That's when the sheriff showed up.

"What's goin' on?"

Clint turned, saw the man with the badge approaching them.

"Just a disagreement, Sheriff."

The man stopped and looked down at the two dead men.

Then he looked at Clint. He looked to be in his forties, probably had a few years behind the badge.

"I knew them," he said.

"If you knew them, then you know they weren't part of a very friendly bunch."

"No, they weren't."

"The others just rode out."

"I might have to talk to them," the sheriff said. "To find out what happened."

"I'm sure there are plenty of men in the saloon who could help you."

"I knew them," the lawman said again, "but I don't know you."

"Then I'll bet you don't know my friend either," Clint said.

"Friend?"

Clint pointed up at Crapface, who was still holding his rifle ready. Since the four ranch hands had ridden out of town, Clint waved at Crapface to come down, then looked at the lawman.

"I think I could use a name from you," the sheriff said.

"My name's Clint Adams, Sheriff," Clint said. "That's my friend, Tyrone Jones."

"Well," the sheriff said, "the Gunsmith. Maybe that's all the explanation I need."

"Why don't we go to your office," Clint said. "Maybe my friend and I could make it clear."

Crapface had made his way down to the street and was approaching the two men.

"All right," the sheriff said, "we'll go to my office, but I'll need to get these bodies off the street first."

SEVEN

After the sheriff got some men to take the bodies over to the undertaker, he led Clint and Crapface to his office. Once inside, he went around behind his desk and sat down.

"Lukas and his bunch are kind of wild," the lawman said. "But I don't know that they deserved to die in the street like that."

"Any man who braces me in the street and won't back down deserves to die in the street," Clint said. "They had plenty of chances to change their minds. The other four were in hiding, but they were smarter. They decided to take the chance I gave them to leave."

"And him?" the sheriff asked.

"It all started with me," Crapface said. "Them six wanted to do to me what I heard they did to you."

That caused the sheriff to bristle, but he didn't deny anything.

"I wasn't about to take a beatin'," Crapface said. "Clint stepped in to help me."

"Did you fellas ride in together?"

"No," Clint said. "We just happen to be going in the same direction."

"You mean this was a coincidence?"

Clint made a face and said, "Yes."

"I'm gonna have to explain to Mr. Jeffson how two of his men got killed."

"Mr. Jeffson?" Clint said.

"He owns the ranch where all them boys work."

"Well then, they'll tell him what happened," Clint said.

"Yeah, maybe," the sheriff said. "Maybe they'll tell him one thing, and I'll tell them another. I'll just let him know how it really happened."

"You want us to go with you?" Clint asked.

The sheriff looked at Crapface and made a face, as if the smell was getting to him.

"No," he said. "That's okay. You fellas just better move on."

"Just like that?" Clint asked.

"Yeah, pretty much," the sheriff said. "I believe you about how things happened. I know how Lukas and them boys operate. So you fellas can just mount up and ride out."

Clint looked at Crapface.

"It suits me," the buffalo hunter said.

Clint looked at the lawman and said, "Okay, then." He stood up. "We'll ride out."

"Good."

The sheriff and Crapface also stood.

"But I've got one thing to say," Clint went on.

"What's that?" the lawman asked.

"If I ever find out there's paper out on either one of us,

that we're wanted—I'll be coming back here for you. Understand?"

"I get it," the sheriff said. "Don't worry, I won't cross you."

"Make sure you don't."

Clint and Crapface walked to the door, and Clint looked back at the man standing behind the desk.

"Don't worry," the sheriff said. "I'll take care of everything."

"See that you do."

Outside Crapface said, "You think he'll keep his word?"

"I think he will."

"But you still wanna stay around?"

"No," Clint said. "I don't. If we stay, this could drag on for a long time."

"So then we better get out of here. Where's your horse?"

"In front of the saloon."

"Mine, too," Crapface said. "Let's go."

They walked to the saloon, mounted up, and rode out of town.

After a few miles Crapface asked, "Where are you headed?"

"Don't know," Clint said.

"Then come with me."

"To the panhandle?"

"To hunt buffalo," Crapface said. "Again. How long has it been?"

"A long time."

"So?"

Clint studied his friend for a few moments, then shrugged and said, "Why not?"

EIGHT

When they saw the buildings in the distance, they reined in. It had been two weeks since they left Walton, Nebraska.

"Not supposed to be any towns around here," Crapface said. "Southwestern part of Kansas ain't supposed to have no towns."

"Maybe it's not a town," Clint said.

"That many buildings?" Crapface asked. "That high? We can see 'em from here—they're two stories high."

"Doesn't matter much," Clint said. "After all, we're just going to be passing through."

"We was passing through Walton, too, wasn't we?" the buffalo hunter asked. "Found us some trouble there, didn't we?"

"Well, you did," Clint said.

Crapface looked at him and grinned.

"Couldn't keep your big nose outta my business, couldja?"

"I never can," Clint said, "when I see a friend of mine being a damn fool."

"What?"

"You could've backed down some from those guys," Clint said.

"And let them dunk me in a trough?"

"Well, not that far," Clint said. "But some."

"I don't back down from fools like that," Crapface said. "If that makes me a fool, I can't help it."

They sat their horses and stared at the buildings in the distance.

"We could go around," Crapface said.

"We could use some supplies," Clint said. "And I could use a beer and a steak."

"Sounds good to me," Crapface said.

"So let's ride up ahead and see what we find," Clint suggested.

"But just to eat and stock up, right?" Crapface said. "I don't wanna be there long enough to stir up trouble."

"Crapface," Clint said, "since when did it take you more than five minutes to stir up some trouble?"

"What happened in Nebraska waren't my fault!" the buffalo hunter complained as they started forward . . .

When they reached the buildings, they saw that there were only a few of them. The rest of the town was made up of tents and shacks. Clint had seen many boomtowns start this way—Dodge City, Leadville, and many others. As they rode down the pitted main street, there were people all around them.

"What's booming around here?" Clint asked. "There are no mines, no buffalo, no rail . . ."

"Maybe we can find out while we get a drink," Crapface said.

"Good thought."

They found a saloon housed in a large tent. There was a crudely erected bar inside, with two bartenders working it. There were barrels and crates being used as tables, some wooden chairs and stools around them.

Clint and Crapface walked to the bar.

"Ho, friend," one of the bartenders said to Crapface, "that's a pretty ripe scent you're carryin' around with you."

Crapface looked aggrieved and asked, "How do you know it's me?"

"I think those skins might have been a good tip-off," the man said. "What can I get you gents?"

"A couple of beers," Clint said.

"Comin' up."

When he put them down in front of them. Clint was surprised to see they were ice cold.

"Can you tell us where we are?" Clint asked.

"Sure thing. The town is called Woodsdale."

"And it is a town?" Clint asked.

"Well . . . almost. We haven't been officially recognized yet, but that's bein' worked on."

"By who?" Crapface asked.

"Well, I guess you'd call them our town fathers," the bartender said.

"But why would someone put a town—" Clint started.

"'Scuse me," the barman said, and went off to serve another customer.

"Sounds like he may not wanna talk about it," Crapface said.

"Maybe not."

Crapface sniffed the air.

"You don't have a problem with the way I smell, do ya?"

"Not really," Clint said. "But then I've been around buffalo before."

"You sayin' buffalo stink?"

"I'm saying," Clint said, "that everybody's smells take getting used to."

"But—"

"Drink your beer."

NINE

They nursed their beers, watched the comings and goings in the saloon. They heard some conversations, mostly about some list of names that was being prepared. Men were being asked if they had signed their names yet. Others said they had just come from signing.

They ordered a second beer each when a man in a suit and bowler hat entered. He started flitting about from table to table, man to man, asking the same question.

"Have you signed . . . have you signed . . . have you signed?"

Eventually, he reached Clint and Crapface. He recoiled from the buffalo hunter for a moment, then held his sleeve up in front of his face.

"Have you gents signed?"

"Signed what?" Clint asked.

"We're asking all the citizens of Woodsdale to register *as* citizens."

"Why?" Crapface asked.

"It will help us when it comes to being named the county seat."

"If you're the only town around here, why would there be a problem being named the county seat?" Clint asked.

Now the man made a face that had nothing to do with Crapface's scent.

"We're not the only town," he said. "Hugoton is also trying to get named the county seat."

"And this is a new county?" Clint asked.

"Ain't even been named yet," the man said. "How about it, gents? We need as many names as we can get."

"But we ain't citizens," Crapface said.

"That's okay," the man said. "All you have to do is sign. And if you know some other names, like friends or family, you can put them down, too."

"That doesn't sound legal," Clint said.

"Well, since there isn't any law here yet, that really doesn't matter, does it?"

"I don't think I'm comfortable with that," Clint said.

"Me neither," Crapface said.

"Well, if you change your mind, come on over to the City Hall. We've already erected a few buildings, and that's one of them. I'm Mitch Fielding, by the way, and I'm one of the town fathers. I work with the colonel." The man extended his hand to Clint.

"We'll keep it in mind," Clint said, shaking Fielding's hand.

"Have a good day," the man said, not extending his hand to Crapface. Then he moved on, stopping to talk to others along the way.

"Whataya think of that?" Crapface asked.

"I've seen it done before," Clint said, "in other towns.

Battles over being named the county seat have gotten very ugly."

"Why? What's the difference?"

"It's all political, Crapface," Clint said. "Being the mayor of the county seat is supposed to be very prestigious."

"Politicians," Crapface said. "And they say I stink!"

TEN

The day dragged on, then suddenly a couple of saloon girls appeared to work the floor of the tented saloon. With the girls circulating among the customers, business began to pick up. Finally, a couple of poker games broke out on some hastily constructed larger tables. Basically, the games were being played on top of large sections of wood balanced on some barrels.

"Don't even think about it," Crapface said.

"What?"

"I know how you are with women and poker, Clint," the buffalo hunter said. "We're only supposed to be here to get something to eat and some supplies, and we ain't ate yet."

"Well then, we better get a move on," Clint said. "Let's go find some steaks, and then pick up a few supplies."

They finished their beers and set the empty mugs down on the bar.

"Leavin' so soon?" one of the girls asked, coming up to

Clint. She was a pretty blonde about twenty-five, with blue eyes and beautiful smooth, pale skin.

"Just to get something to eat," Clint said. "Do you know a place that can do a good steak?"

"Just go next door," she said. "It's owned by my boss, and it's got good food. I eat there all the time. Make sure you have some pie after."

"Okay," Clint said. "What's your name?"

"Penny."

"I'll come back and let you know how we liked it, Penny," he said.

She was a little short so she reached up to pull his ear down to her.

"When you come back, leave your smelly friend outside," she whispered, and then flicked his ear with her silken tongue.

He smiled at her and followed Crapface outside.

"What'd she say?" the buffalo hunter asked.

"She told me to eat next door."

"I heard that part," the smaller man said. "What'd she say about me?"

"What makes you think she said anything about you?" Clint asked.

"Come on," Crapface said, "she said somethin' about the way I smell."

"She said they had steaks next door," Clint said, "and I'm going over there to find out."

Crapface hurried after Clint, still demanding to know what the girl had said . . .

"Well," Clint said later, "she was right about the steaks."

Crapface had been pretty quiet during the meal of steak and vegetables.

"Come on," Clint said, "stop worry about what the pretty girl said about you."

"I mean," Crapface said, "I know I got a smell, but it ain't that bad . . . is it?"

Clint looked around them. The other people in the tent had moved away from them, so there were empty tables around them.

"No," Clint said, "it's not that bad."

That seemed to mollify Crapface a bit. Clint waved at the middle-aged waitress until she reluctantly came over. She stood on his side of the table, next to him.

"Sir?"

"I'm told you have great pie."

She brightened up and said, "Yes, sir. My husband makes several kinds a day."

"What kinds do you have today?"

"Apple and rhubarb . . . oh, and peach."

Clint smiled. "My favorite! I'll have the peach."

"Rhubarb for me," Crapface said.

"And coffee," Clint added.

"Yes, sir."

She grabbed their empty plates and went off for the pie.

"Rhubarb?" Clint asked.

"What? I like it."

"Why doesn't that surprise me?"

Crapface decided to change the subject.

"We gotta get some supplies after this and then get goin'," he said.

"Well, I want to go back next door for a little while."

"What for? Poker or the girl?"

"I just want to tell her she was right about the food here."

"Clint," Crapface said, "I'm surprised you ain't been killed by now because of some woman."

Clint laughed and admitted, "It's not like I haven't come close."

ELEVEN

They left the restaurant tent, completely satisfied with their meal, right down to the pie and coffee.

"We need to find the supply tent," Crapface said.

"I'll look in the saloon," Clint said.

"There ain't no supplies in there."

"Maybe the girl, Penny, will know where to go," Clint said, heading for the saloon tent.

"Clint—"

"I'll meet you in here," Clint said, "after you pick up some supplies."

"Which I'm payin' for?"

"Hey," Clint said, "the whole buffalo hunt was your idea, right?"

Crapface said something, but Clint didn't hear it as he went into the saloon.

The place was much busier than it had been before. Three girls were working the floor. He walked to the bar, where the same bartender stepped up to serve him.

"Beer?"

"Yes."

"Where's your friend?" the man asked, setting the beer in front of him. "Not that I miss him. Sheesh, what a smell. I'm just curious."

"He's buying supplies."

"Gonna be on your way?"

"Pretty soon."

"Headin' where?"

Clint decided to be vague.

"South, I guess. Who knows?"

He turned with his beer and saw that the same man with the suit and bowler was working the crowd again.

"Is he still looking for signatures?" he asked.

"Oh, yeah," the barman said. "He's one of them town fathers. He works with the colonel. The more names he can get, the better, ya know?"

"Even if he has to make them up?"

"He don't make 'em up," the bartender said, "but he don't care if other people do."

"Ah."

Clint looked around again.

"Lookin' for somebody?"

"Penny," he said, just as he saw her across the tent.

"Oh," the bartender said. "You like her?"

"I don't know her."

"That can be fixed," the barman said. "For a price."

Clint looked at him.

"What's your name?"

"Brent."

"Well, Brent, I don't pay women to have sex with me."

"Never?"

"Never."

Brent studied Clint for a few moments, then said, "Well, maybe you don't have to."

Clint looked at Brent, who was fairly young, kind of gangly, with a mop of unruly blond hair.

"No," Clint said, "I don't. Not usually."

"You're a lucky man."

The bar was busy, so Brent had to move along, which suited Clint. He turned and saw Penny waling toward him. She had changed from the simple dress she'd been wearing earlier to a red gown that showed off her pale shoulders.

"You came back."

"I wanted to tell you that you were right," Clint said.

"Good steak?" she asked.

"And pie."

"See? I would never steer you wrong. Are you lookin' for a place to stay?"

"No," Clint said, "my partner and I figure to move on."

"Today? It's gettin' late."

"We'll camp along the way."

"You'll miss out on all the comforts we have to offer," she warned.

He looked her up and down and said, "I'm sure the comforts are impressive, but we really do need to be on our way."

"That's too bad."

"We need some supplies," Clint said. "Not a lot, just a few things."

"Well, just go out the front, make a right, walk two blocks, and then cross over. There's a tent there with everything you'll need."

"Much obliged."

"But finish your beer first," she said, putting her hand on his arm. "Don't rush away."

"I'm not rushing," he assured her.

She rubbed his arm and said, "Maybe I can even convince you to let me freshen that with a cold one."

He looked at the half a mug of beer he was holding in his hand and said, "Maybe."

TWELVE

Crapface Jones entered the general store tent and began to prowl the makeshift shelves. He'd shopped for supplies in boomtown stores like this before. The prices were usually high, but negotiable. He and Clint didn't need a lot, just some coffee, bacon, flour so he could make some biscuits, sugar, beef jerky—small things that added up. Crapface was not well educated, but he did his sums very well. When he knew how much he was buying and how much it would cost, he approached the counter and prepared himself to dicker.

There were two men at the counter already, and they were not only dickering, they were arguing.

"You gotta be kiddin' me," one of them said. "We're buyin' coffee, not gold dust."

"Sorry, gents," the clerk said, "but that's the price. There are lots of folks hereabouts buying coffee."

"And how can you be selling these penny stogies for a nickel?" the other man asked. "These sure as hell ain't nickel cigars."

"They are around here," the clerk said. He was a tall, slender man in his forties, wearing a white apron that covered him almost from neck to toe.

The two men arguing with him were wearing trail clothes, and looked as if they had just recently ridden into town.

Suddenly one of them raised his chin and sniffed the air.

"Jesus, what is that smell?"

"It ain't my store," the clerk said.

The two men looked at each other, then turned and looked at Crapface.

"Christ," the other one said, "what the hell are you?"

"I'm tryin' to buy some supplies, if you fellas would get on with your transaction. Or stand aside."

"Stand aside?" one of them asked. "Who you tellin' to stand aside? We was here first."

"Fine," Crapface said, "then finish doin' what you're doin' so I can get outta here."

Now the two men turned to face him. They towered over him, which did not intimidate him, but emboldened them.

"Look, friend," one of them said, "why don't you wait outside so you don't stink up the place."

"This is how you let folks talk to your customers?" Crapface asked the clerk. "What if I decide to buy my supplies somewhere else?"

"Good luck," the clerk said. "There ain't no other place in town."

"So you want my money?" Crapface asked.

"Sure, I do. But these gents were here first."

"I got no problem with that," Crapface said. He took a deep breath and made a decision that went against the grain. "Why don't I just wait outside 'til their done?"

"That's what we're sayin'," one of the men said.

"Yeah," the other one said, "take the stink outside."

Crapface thought about getting out of this situation without any trouble. He didn't want Clint saying he couldn't go anywhere without starting trouble.

"I'll come back when they're finished," he told the clerk.

"Fine, thanks," the clerk said.

"Yeah, you better leave," one of the men muttered as Crapface went outside.

"Jesus," Tim Santee said to his partner, Micah McCain. "That smell is still in here."

"Let's get our supplies and get out of here," McCain said.

"I think we should finish here and then go outside and beat the snot outta that runt," Santee said.

"Why?" McCain asked.

"I don't know," Santee said. "I just think I need to kick the shit outta somebody."

"We'd have to watch out for the buffalo shooter he's carryin'," McCain said.

"He don't have a chance against our handguns," Santee said. "We just take it away from him."

The clerk reappeared with their supplies, set them down on the counter.

"We all set on prices?" he asked them.

"Yeah, but you're gougin' us," Santee said.

"'Cause you're the only place in town," McCain said.

They kept complaining even as they handed over their money.

"Let's get this stuff on the packhorse and get to that little buffalo hunter," Santee said.

"Why don't we wait for him to do his business and come

out," McCain said. "We can get the drop on him that way and get that rifle away from him."

"Good idea," Santee said, filling his arms with supplies. "Let's go."

THIRTEEN

Crapface saw the two men come out, their arms loaded down with supplies, and go to their packhorse. His instinct was to get the drop on them and disarm them. Instead, he went into the tent.

"You got a list?" the clerk asked.

"No," Crapface said, "but I know what I want. Can we talk price?"

The clerk sniffed the air.

"Why not? Faster we deal, the faster you leave. You really do smell, you know."

Crapface took a deep breath, then started telling the clerk what he needed.

Crapface came out of the tent carrying the supplies in a burlap sack in one hand, and his rifle in the other.

"Hold it right there, Smelly," a voice said.

Crapface stopped, realizing he should have followed his

instincts. These guys were looking for trouble, and just happened to find him. Not his fault.

Clint came out of the saloon, sorry that they weren't staying in town overnight because he knew Penny was available to him. He started to follow her directions to where he figured Crapface was buying supplies, and that's when he heard the shot. He knew the sound of a Big Fifty when he heard it.

He broke into a run, saw the three men struggling in front of the tent. Crapface swung his Sharps and struck one man on the shoulder, knocking him aside. He continued to struggle with the second man. As Clint got closer, he saw the first man swing around with his gun out.

"Don't!" he shouted, drawing his gun.

The man either ignored him or didn't hear him. He pointed his gun at the two struggling men, and Clint fired. As his bullet struck the man in the chest, his gun discharged, still pointed at Crapface and the other man.

The bullet hit one of them and the two men fell apart. Crapface staggered, tripped over his fallen rifle. The other man drew his gun, giving Clint no choice but to fire again.

He ran to Crapface, saw that his friend was bleeding from a shoulder wound.

"Are you okay?" he asked, crouching over him.

"No, I ain't okay!" the buffalo hunter snapped. "It hurts like hell!"

Others came running, surrounded them and the other two fallen men.

"They're dead," someone said.

"Who killed them?" another asked.

"That feller."

They turned and looked at Clint and Crapface.

"It waren't my fault!" Crapface said.

FOURTEEN

While the onlooker gaped at them, Clint shouted, "He needs a doctor!"

Nobody said anything.

"Is there a doctor in this damn town?" he yelled.

"Um, yeah, we got one," a man said. He was in his thirties, not wearing a gun or a hat. Looked like he had just come out from behind a store counter.

"Help me."

The man hesitated, but Clint still had his gun in his hand, so the man stooped to help lift Crapface to his feet.

"Oh, God," he said, "what's that stench?"

"Take us to the doctor!" Clint snapped.

The doctor was set up in a small tent. He took Crapface inside, then turned and put his hand on Clint's chest.

"No room, friend," he said. "Wait out here."

Clint nodded. He took the time to reload his gun, and

then holstered it. The man who had helped him carry Crap-face over was still standing there.

"I hear you don't have a sheriff or a marshal in town," Clint said.

"No, sir," the man said, "but that don't mean we don't got any law."

"Oh?"

"We got the colonel."

"Is he the colonel who's got someone collecting signatures?"

"Yup. Colonel Samuel Hewitt Woods."

"Woods, as in . . ."

"Woodsdale."

"I see."

"You killed those other two."

"I had no choice."

A young man came running up to them, carrying Crap-face's rifle.

"I figured your friend would want this back," he said, handing Clint the Sharps.

"Thanks. Did you see what happened?"

"Yeah," the man said, "them other two jumped your friend as he came out of Daily's."

"Daily's?"

"Yeah, that tent he was in was Daily's Supplies."

"Okay," Clint said, "I'm going to ask you to stay here with me."

"Why?" the young man asked.

"Because he's going to go and get your Colonel Woods and bring him here," Clint said. He turned to the other man and said, "Go!"

"Yes, sir."

The man ran off and Clint turned to the younger man again.

"How'd you come to see what happened?" Clint asked.

"I was passin' by, saw your friend walkin' outta Daily's, carryin' a burlap bag and that Sharps rifle. Great-lookin' gun!"

"Yes, it is."

"I saw them stop him. He pulled the trigger on his rifle, scared the shit outta them. That's when they jumped him. He was doin' pretty good for a while. I was impressed, him bein' so small."

"Did it ever occur to you to help him?"

"I don't have no gun, mister."

"Right," Clint said. "Okay, look, run back to Daily's and find me that burlap bag, then come back here. I want you to tell your story to this Colonel Woods."

"Okay."

The kid ran off at the same moment the doctor stepped out of his tent. He was wiping his hands on a rag. He had a series of wrinkles on his face that Clint used to guess his age at about fifty.

"How's he doing?"

"I got the bullet out," the doctor said. "He'll be okay. Can you get him to take a bath?"

"For any reason other than the smell?" Clint asked.

"It just might help ward off infection," the sawbones said.

"Okay, I'll see to it that he does. Can he ride?"

"Not for a few days," the doc said. "You try and he'll bleed out."

"Damn," Clint said. "Is there anyplace to stay in town?"

"Got a few tents with cots set up in them," the doctor said, "and the new hotel."

"Hotel?"

"One of the first buildings they put up," the doctor said.

"Think they have any rooms left?"

"Plenty," the man said. "It's kind of expensive."

"I'll have to risk it."

"Give him some time to rest and then you can walk him over."

"That's okay," Clint said. "I've got to wait here for Colonel Woods."

"What for?"

"I heard he's the law—or the closest thing to it."

"He's got a candidate he's supporting for sheriff," the doctor said.

"Who would that be?"

"John Cross."

"Haven't met him."

"Well, now's your chance," the doctor said. "Here they come."

Clint turned, saw the man he'd sent to find the colonel walking toward him with two men.

"What's your name, Doc?"

"Hammond."

"How much I owe you?"

"I'll let you know."

They shook hands and the doc went back into his tent.

Clint turned to face the oncoming Colonel Woods and his choice for sheriff, John Cross.

FIFTEEN

"Colonel Woods?" Clint said as the men reached him.

The older man—about sixty, with wavy gray hair—said, "That's me. This is future Sheriff John Cross."

"Future?" Clint looked at Cross, tall, about forty-five, wore his gun as if he knew how to handle it. He had a jaw that looked like it had been carved out of granite.

"It's assured," Woods said. "This feller here said you wanted to see us?"

"Can I go?" the man asked.

"Sure," Clint said. "Thanks for your help." He turned his attention to Woods and Cross. "There was a shooting over by Daily's."

"I heard about that," Cross said in his deep voice. His mouth barely moved when he spoke. "That was you?"

"That was my friend, and then I came along and kind of saved his life."

"By killing a man?" Cross asked.

"Two men."

"Oh, two men," the future sheriff said. "You came to our town and killed two men?"

"To save my friend."

"He's in there?" Cross asked, indicating the doctor's tent.

"Yes."

"Go and talk to him, Cross," Woods said, "I'll continue to speak with Mr. . . ."

"Adams."

"With Mr. Adams."

Cross studied Clint for a moment, then ducked inside the tent.

"Adams?" Woods asked. "And your first name?"

"Clint."

"Ah . . ." he said. "Now I understand."

"Do you?"

"Perhaps not," Woods said, "but it doesn't matter. I think perhaps we could help each other, Mr. Adams."

"Oh? How?"

"Well," Woods said, "for one thing, I'll keep you and your friend out of jail."

"You have a jail?"

Woods smiled.

"I was speaking metaphorically," he said. "I can keep you from being detained. I can also make sure you are comfortable."

"The hotel?"

Woods nodded.

"Free," he said.

"And what do I need to do in return?"

"We can discuss that," Woods said, "over some dinner tonight."

"But now?"

"For now," Woods said, "I'll call Cross off."

"It was self-defense, with witnesses," Clint said.

"Perhaps . . ."

John Cross came out of the tent. Woods gave a slight shake of his head so that he would not speak in front of Clint.

"What do you say, sir?" Woods asked. "Dinner?"

"The wounded man can't ride," Cross said.

"He'll need a place to rest," Woods said, and added, "someplace comfortable."

"All right," Clint said. "We'll need two rooms."

"Done. Someone will come for you at dinnertime."

"Fine."

"Cross," Woods said to his future sheriff, "let's go and talk."

The two men turned and walked away. Clint ducked into the doctor's tent.

SIXTEEN

Clint walked Crapface over to the hotel, where two rooms were waiting for them. The clerk wrinkled his nose as he gave Clint two keys.

"Wow," Crapface said as Clint walked him into his room. "How did you get us these rooms?"

"I don't know," Clint said. "I haven't agreed to anything yet but dinner. Oh, and a bath."

"For you?"

"For you."

"Why?"

"The doctor says it will help ward off any infection."

Clint helped Crapface get his skins off, and then got him into a seated position on the bed.

"Don't get beneath the sheets yet," he said. "Not until you're clean."

"And when will that happen?"

There was a knock on the door.

"Now," Clint said.

He opened the door carefully, then swung it open. Two men entered, each holding two buckets of hot water.

"What are they gonna do with that?" Crapface asked fearfully.

"There's a tub in every room," Clint said. "They're going to get it ready for you. Are you going to need help getting in?"

"I can get into a tub by myself!" Crapface said.

"Have you ever done it before?"

"I've had baths before, Clint."

"In a tub?"

"Well . . . in a lake, a waterhole . . . in a water tower once."

"But never in a real bathtub?"

"Well . . . no."

"It's not hard," Clint said. "Just don't get that bandage wet."

"Yeah, okay."

The room door was open and two more men walked in carrying buckets.

"Jesus," Crapface said, "are they lookin' ta drown me?"

Clint went to his room to have a bath of his own. He didn't hear any screaming from Crapface's room, so he assumed his friend was doing okay in all that hot water.

He was in the tub when there was a knock at the door. He sighed, grabbed the gun from the chair he'd set next to the tub, then padded nude to the door. Whoever it was deserved a little shock for interrupting his bath.

"This better be good—" he said, then stopped short when he saw who was in the hall.

"Well," Penny said, "from where I stand, it looks pretty good."

She looked him up and down, smiling, obviously pleased with what she saw. She still had on the dress she'd been wearing in the saloon.

Clint decided not to be shy.

"And what brings you here?" he asked. "Aren't you supposed to be working?"

"I have a little time off," she said. "Guess how I thought I'd spend it?"

She moved close to him, reached between his legs, and gave him a stroke.

He grabbed her in a wet embrace, pulled her into the room, and slammed the door.

SEVENTEEN

Clint undressed Penny very quickly, picked her up in his arms, and carried her to the tub. She screamed as he dropped her in, and then got in with her.

She was not a big girl, and fit in the tub with him very well. Her body was tight, with small but solid breasts, taut, silky buttocks.

He reached for her nipples, tweaked them until they were hard. Meanwhile, she took hold of his wet penis and pulled on it with one hand while sliding her other hand beneath his balls to fondle and tickle him.

He pulled her close then, to kiss her, pinning his erection between them. She giggled against his mouth, rubbed her hairy public patch over his cock, moaning. He switched to her breasts, sucking the nipples into his mouth and then biting them. She may have had small breasts, but her distended nipples were long and sensitive.

They kissed, and explored each other with their hands, until suddenly Penny moved away from him, turned, and stood. She braced both hands on the edge of the tub and lifted her butt to him. He knew what she wanted and he was more than willing—and ready—to give it to her.

He got behind her, held his penis in his hand, and eased it into her from behind. Her hands tightened on the edge of the tub, and he took hold of her hips and started to take her in long, slow strokes. She moaned—it was almost a humming sound— as he took her, slowly at first, then faster until she was lunging back against him and they were splashing the floor with water.

He ran his right hand up her back and let it rest on the nape of her neck. With his left hand he reached around and fondled her while he continued to fuck her. Eventually, her body began to tremble, her legs stiffened, and she cried out just as he exploded into her . . .

When he dried himself off, he dressed in the same clothes. He had nothing else that was clean, wondered if he'd be able to buy some decent clothes here in Woodsdale. Even if he could, he didn't have time before someone would come to take him to have dinner with Colonel Samuel Hewitt Woods.

Penny lay on the bed, exhausted. The sheets were wet as she had flopped onto the bed right from the tub, watched him dry off and get dressed.

"I thought you had a break and had to go back to work," he said.

"What can they do," she replied, "fire me? I'll go back soon. Or maybe I'll just wait here for you to come back."

"It's up to you."

He leaned over her, kissed the back of her damp neck, and then one of her dimples above her butt.

"I'll see you whenever," he said.

"Mmm," she said.

* * *

He went across the hall to check on Crapface. When he knocked, the buffalo hunter yelled out, "It ain't locked!"

Clint entered. Crapface was lying on the bed, but not beneath the sheets. He was wearing soiled long johns and nothing else. And remarkably, he didn't smell. The room did, though, because his skins were heaped in a corner, but Clint could tell the smell wasn't coming from the man himself.

"Amazing."

"What?" Crapface asked.

"This is what you look like under all those skins?" Clint asked.

Crapface looked down at himself.

"What's wrong with me?"

"Nothing," Clint said, "except that without the skins, you look about fifty pounds lighter."

"Maybe that's why I wear 'em then," Crapface said. "So I won't get picked on."

"But you get picked on *because* you wear them," Clint pointed out.

"Yeah, but maybe less."

The long johns were bloody around the wound.

"I'll get you some new underwear," Clint said. "Maybe get us each some new shirts."

"How about some food?"

"I'll have some sent up."

"Somethin' good."

"Steak."

"Two steaks," Crapface said. "I gotta get my strength back."

"Okay."

"You gonna eat with that colonel guy?"

"Yes, dinner."

"The other fella, the almost sheriff? I told him the story. Now I gotta thank you for savin' my life."

"I didn't have anything else to do."

"It wasn't my fault, Clint."

"I know it," Clint said. "Don't worry."

"Yeah, okay."

"Hello?"

Clint had left the door open, and now a man was sticking his head in.

"Yep?" he said.

"Um, I was sent to fetch a man named Clint Adams," the young man said. It was the same young man Clint had sent to get the burlap bag of supplies Crapface had dropped.

"You owe me a bag," Clint said.

"Um, yeah, I got it. But the colonel told me ta get lost."

"Well, leave it at the desk for me."

"Yessir, I surely will."

"Okay," Clint said, "now take me to the colonel."

"Yessir."

Clint turned to Crapface.

"I'll see you later."

"Watch yerself," the buffalo hunter said. "There's still some buffalo waitin' for us."

"They'll wait," Clint said.

"I hope so."

Clint headed for the door, said over his shoulder, "I'll send up those steaks."

"Yeah, and have a pretty girl bring 'em up," Crapface yelled back.

EIGHTEEN

The young man led Clint to a large tent. Inside a table had been set for dinner, and the colonel was sitting there, drinking wine or brandy out of a crystal glass.

"Come in, Mr. Adams," Woods said. "Brandy?"

"Sure, why not?"

Clint looked around while the colonel poured the brandy himself. John Cross was nowhere to be seen."

Woods approached Clint and handed him the glass, said to the young man, "Tell the cook to start serving."

"Yessir."

He started out, but Clint said, Wait."

Woods looked at him.

"My friend is hungry. I'd like someone to bring him a couple of steaks."

"A couple?" Woods asked, laughing.

"That's right."

Woods looked at the young man.

"Have someone take two steak dinners up to the gentleman."

"Preferably a pretty girl."

"Anything else?" Woods asked.

"Now that you ask, a new pair of long johns and two new shirts."

"You heard him."

"Yessir."

The young man left the tent.

"Come, have a seat, Mr. Adams."

Clint approached the table, saw two settings.

"Mr. Cross will not be joining us?" he asked.

"Maybe for coffee," Woods said. "I hope you like chicken."

Clint preferred steak, but he said, "Chicken's fine."

Clint sat. A man wearing an apron came out and stood next to the colonel.

"We'll start with the soup," Woods said.

"Yessir."

"Then after the chicken Mr. Cross will be joining us for coffee and dessert."

"Yessir."

"You can start serving."

As the cook left, Woods looked down the long table at Clint.

"How is your friend doing, by the way?"

"He's okay," Clint said. "Just hungry."

"Well, we're taking care of that, aren't we?"

"Yes, we are."

"I don't suppose you were able to convince him to take a bath?"

"As a matter of fact, I was."

"Excellent."

"He still has those skins, though. Not much I could do about that."

"Oh. How do you stand it?"

"I've hunted a lot of buffalo," Clint said. "You get used to the smell. In fact, sometimes it gets so you miss it."

"I've never hunted buffalo myself."

"It's not an experience you would ever forget."

Two waiters came in and served them their soup.

"Onion," Woods said. "There are plenty of them growing wild along the Cimarron."

Clint tasted it.

"It's excellent."

"Thank you. I brought Oscar with me, first to McPherson, and now here."

"Oscar?"

"The cook."

Clint knew that McPherson was a town in Kansas, probably eight or ten miles from where they were.

"I am part of a syndicate that formed in McPherson to build this county, and this town."

"Someone told me about another town near here."

Woods bristled.

"That would be Hugoton," he said. "They're competing with us for the county seat, but they won't get it."

"How can you be sure?"

"We're going to end up with the larger constituency," Woods said. "And we'll have the county sheriff."

"Mr. Cross."

"Yes," Woods said. "He's ex-military, has worn a badge in Arizona and Texas."

"He seems competent enough."

"However," Woods said, "we would probably be in an even better position if we had you on our side?"

"Me?"

"Yes," Woods said. "Your name, and your gun."

"I don't hire out my gun," Clint said.

"We don't have to call you a gun for hire," Woods said as the waiters appeared with steaming plates. "But we can discuss that after dinner. Shall we?"

The waiter set Clint's plate down in front of him.

"Yes, let's," Clint said.

NINETEEN

The dinner was delicious. While they were eating, one of the waiters came out and set a fourth place at the table.

"A fourth?" Clint asked Woods.

"I wasn't sure whether or not our fourth would join us, but apparently we're in luck."

The waiters cleared the empty plates, poured some more brandy for Woods and Clint.

"We have cherry pie for dessert," Woods said. "My favorite."

Clint nodded. Cherry was his least favorite, but that didn't matter much.

At that moment John Cross walked in, removed his hat.

"Ah, Sheriff Cross."

"Sheriff?" Clint asked. "A little premature, isn't it?"

"Not at all," Woods said. "As I told you, it's almost a foregone conclusion."

"Except for Sam Robinson," Cross said, seating himself.

"Who's Robinson?"

"He owns the saloon," Woods said. "And he wants to be sheriff."

"Is there going to be an election?" Clint asked.

"Well, of course," Woods said. "A fair, democratic election."

Clint looked at Cross.

"Which you're going to win."

Cross shrugged.

"With you on the ticket as his deputy," Woods said, "he'd be a shoo-in."

"That would be a no," Clint said.

"All right," Woods said, "then we'll just put you on my payroll. What's your price?"

"To do what?"

"To help us be named the county seat."

"That sounds like a political problem," Clint said. "I don't get involved in politics."

"Well," Woods said, "it involves a little more than politics."

"Like what?"

"Guns," Cross said.

One waiter came in and asked if they should serve the coffee and pie.

"Not yet," Colonel Woods said. "We're waiting for our fourth to arrive."

"Oh, she has arrived, sir," the waiter said.

"Has she? Then by all means, serve dessert."

"Yessir."

"She?" Clint asked.

"My daughter," Woods said. "Ah, here she is."

She came through the front flap of the tent, a vision in lavender, cut to show off her shoulders and cleavage.

"My dear," Woods said, standing.

Cross leaped to his feet and straightened his back.

"Joyce," he said. "How wonderful to see you."

"John," she said, "Father. And who is this handsome man?"

She stopped by Clint's chair, giving him a good whiff of her perfume. He dropped his napkin on the table and stood up.

"My name is Clint Adams, Miss Woods."

"A pleasure," she said, extending her hand. He took it, held it briefly, and released it.

"Joyce, please take a seat. Dessert is being served."

"Thank you, Father," she said.

Before Clint could move, Cross ran around the table and held her chair for her.

"Thank you, John."

Cross hurried back to his own chair, sat directly across from the beautiful brunette.

"Mr. Adams, are you working with my father and Sheriff Cross?"

"I'm not working with your father, Miss Woods," Clint said, "and as far as I know, Mr. Cross is not sheriff yet."

"Oh, but he will be," Joyce said.

"How do you know that?"

"Well . . . my father has told me so," she said. "And so has John."

"Well then," Clint said, "it must be so."

She looked puzzled.

"But why wouldn't it be?"

"It seems to me a man named Sam Robinson might have something to say about it," Clint said. "Or a town called Hugoton."

She looked at the colonel.

"Father?"

"Don't worry, dear," Woods said. "All we need do now is eat our pie and drink our coffee. We won't be discussing business in front of you any longer."

The waiters came in with the pie and coffee, and Clint decided to go along with the colonel.

This time.

TWENTY

After the pie and coffee, Colonel Woods took out three cigars, passed one each to Cross and Clint.

"Well," Joyce said, "if you're going to light those smelly things up, I think I'll take my leave."

She stood, accompanied by all three men.

"Mr. Adams," she said, "it was a pleasure to meet you."

"Joyce, may I see you to your room?" Cross asked.

"Of course, John," she said. "I'd feel so much safer if you would."

"Sir," Cross said to Woods.

"Please, John," Woods said. "I would appreciate it."

Joyce went to her father and kissed him, then said, "Good night, Mr. Adams."

"Good night, Miss Woods."

"Please," she said, "the next time we meet, call me Joyce."

"I will . . . Joyce."

She left, followed by the steely-eyed John Cross, who gave Clint a hard look on the way out.

"Somebody's in love," Clint said to Woods.

"Yes, but I'm afraid it's just Mr. Cross," Woods said. "My daughter has a mind of her own, and is not interested in him."

"Too bad."

"She'll marry him, though."

"How do you know that?"

"It's part of my plan," the colonel said, "and my plans always work."

"Is that a fact?"

"It is a fact, sir," Woods said. "That's why I'd like you to work for me, for Woodsdale. With you on our side, the plan will work."

Clint stood up.

"Colonel," he said, "thanks very much for a great dinner, but I'm afraid I have to disappoint you. Your plan will have to come together without me."

Woods sat back in his chair, puffed on his cigar thoughtfully.

"Think it over, Mr. Adams," he finally said. "I'll pay you very well to work for me. There will be many, many perks."

"I don't have to think it over, Colonel," Clint said, "but thanks anyway. I'm sure we'll see each other around town over the next few days, but after that—after my friend is cleared by the doctor to ride—we'll be leaving."

"Enjoy your stay, Mr. Adams," Woods said.

Clint nodded, turned, and left the tent.

One of the buildings on the edge of town—the first one built—was a house that Colonel Woods had designed for himself and his daughter.

John Cross walked Joyce Woods to the house, where they stopped outside.

"Thank you for seeing me home, John."

"Maybe I could come in for . . . a drink?" he said.

"I don't think so," she said. "I'm rather tired tonight."

"Perhaps another night, then?"

"Yes," she said, "perhaps."

He leaned in to kiss her. She turned her face at the last moment so that his lips landed on her cheek.

"Good night, John."

"Good night, Joyce."

He stood outside and watched until she went in, then turned and walked away.

Joyce went inside, looked out the front window until John Cross was gone. He was a fairly attractive man, but he did not appeal to her. She knew her father wanted her to marry him, but that was not going to happen. For one thing, if and when she did marry, her husband would have to be his own man. He'd have to be able to stand up to the colonel. John Cross would never do that.

Now Clint Adams, there was a man she thought would stand up to her father, and be his own man, without a doubt. She knew his reputation as the Gunsmith, but just during the time she'd sat at the table with him, she could see that he was not impressed, nor was he intimidated, by the colonel.

Clint Adams was definitely a man who appealed to her.

John Cross walked back to the colonel's dining tent, hoping that when he got there, Clint Adams would be gone. He hoped that Adams would not agree to work for the colonel. He had several reasons for this.

First, he didn't think he needed any help to make the colonel's dream come true.

Second, he hadn't liked the way Joyce had been looking at Adams during dinner.

Third, he just plain didn't like the Gunsmith. He wasn't impressed by anyone's reputation, not even his, which was supposed to be legendary. John Cross had faced other men with reputations, and had left them wanting—or dead.

He hoped he could convince the colonel.

Clint walked back to the hotel, hoping that Crapface had gotten his two steak dinners. He was fairly certain the colonel was a man of his word, but failing a simple thing like getting Crapface some food would have changed his mind.

Clint hoped that Colonel Woods would take him at his word that he didn't want to work for him. He was certain John Cross didn't want his help. He could feel the man's dislike coming off him in waves.

On the other hand, he wondered if Cross and Woods could feel what was coming off him and Joyce as they sat at the table together. Clint was surprised the heat hadn't melted the silverware.

He and the beautiful Joyce would be getting together before he left Woodsdale.

When Cross entered the tent, Colonel Woods was still seated at the table, drinking from a wine goblet.

"Is she back home?" he asked.

"Yessir."

"What did you think of Adams?"

"We don't need him."

Woods laughed.

"You don't think so?"

"No, sir."

The colonel looked at his would-be future sheriff.

"I guess we'll find out, John."

"Yes, sir."

Woods lifted his goblet to Cross, who turned and walked out.

TWENTY-ONE

When Clint got to Crapface's room, his friend was just finishing up his second steal dinner. The plate looked like it had been full of meat and potatoes.

"Guess I took care of you," Clint said.

"You sure did," Crapface said. "These was some good steaks."

"They were cooked for you by the colonel's personal chef," Clint said.

"What the hell is a chef?" Crapface asked.

"It's a cook."

"He got his own cook?"

"That's right."

"Well," Crapface said, pushing the second plate to the foot of the bed, where it joined the first one, "he sure got a good one."

Clint took the empties from the bed and put them on a nearby table.

"What'd that colonel want with you, Clint?" Crapface said, trying to settle back comfortably against the bed rail.

"He wants to hire me."

"For what?"

"Not sure," Clint said. "He wants my name, or my gun, or both, to back some kind of play he's making."

"What play?"

"Political, I think."

"You don't wanna get messed up in politics," Crapface said. "I'd rather have somebody come at me with a gun than with some politics."

"I agree," Clint said. "I hate politicians."

"Besides," Crapface said, "what's he need you for, he's got that sheriff of his."

"His future sheriff, you mean."

"He sure of that?"

"He's positive."

Crapface shook his head.

"Politics."

"I'm going to my room for some rest," Clint said. "I'll look in on you later."

"Okay," Crapface said. "I'll be ready to ride tomorrow after some sleep."

"We'll see, Crapface," Clint said. "We'll see."

Clint was reading Mary Shelley's *Frankenstein* when there was a knock on his door.

He slipped his gun from the holster hanging on the bed-post and made his way to the door. He cracked it, saw a man standing in the hall, unarmed. He was tall, about forty-five, wearing a clean suit.

"Mr. Adams?" he said. "Mind if I talk to you?"

"That depends," Clint said. "Who are you?"

"I own this hotel," the man said. "My name's Sam Robinson."

"Mr. Robinson," Clint said. "I've heard of you."

"I'm flattered," Robinson said. "Fact is, I've heard of you, too."

Clint swung the door open and said, "Come on in."

He moved away from the door to let the man enter, put his gun back in its holster.

"Are you happy with your room?" Robinson asked.

"It's a room," Clint said. "A nice room."

"I can get you something bigger."

"Not that I need a bigger room," Clint said, "but why would you do that?"

"To make sure you're comfortable," Robinson said. "You and your friend, that is. Is he all right?"

"He's comfortable."

"That's good."

"And I'm comfortable," Clint said, "but why would you want to make me more comfortable?"

"I understand you had dinner with Colonel Woods tonight," Robinson said. "And Mr. Cross."

"Actually," Clint said, "Mr. Cross only came in for dessert. Along with Miss Woods."

"Ah," Robinson said. "Did you have time to talk business with the colonel?"

"Some."

"I suppose he told you I'm opposing Cross for the job of sheriff?"

"He did," Clint said, "and personally—even though I've only known you a short time—you'd get my vote—if I lived here."

"Well," Robinson said, "maybe we can do something about that."

"I'm afraid not," Clint said. "We'll be leaving very soon."

"At least we can talk tonight."

"About what?"

Robinson looked around.

"How about a drink?" he asked. "I have some wonderful brandy in my office, and we can be comfortable there."

"I'll put on my boots and you can lead the way."

TWENTY-TWO

Robinson's office was on the first floor. It was impressive, larger than most hotel management offices Clint had been in before in Western hotels.

"Have a seat," Robinson said. He poured two glasses of brandy and handed Clint one. Then, instead of sitting behind his desk, he sat in a chair next to Clint's.

"I'm sure the colonel fed you quite a feast," he said, sipping his drink.

"It was quite a spread."

"I'm hoping it will take more than that to impress you."

"Actually," Clint said, "I'm thinking it will take more than you both have to impress me, but by all means, take your best shot."

"Did he offer you money?"

"Lots of it."

"How much?"

"We didn't talk numbers, he just said he'd be generous."

"I can be just as generous."

"Can you?"

"Well . . ." Robinson swirled the brandy in his glass. "I actually don't have the assets the colonel has, but I can get others to back me. Especially with you on my ticket."

"That's not going to happen."

"You haven't heard my offer."

"You can't offer me enough to get involved in politics," Clint said.

"Why not?"

"Politicians are the biggest thieves of all," Clint said. "I'd rather face bank or train robbers."

Robinson sat back.

"Well, it looks like your mind is made up," he said then.

"Besides," Clint said, "we were on our way somewhere when we came here. Just passing through, or so we thought. Now we'll have to wait until my partner heals."

"And what will you do until then?"

"Stay out of trouble . . . I hope."

Robinson raised his glass.

"Here's to keeping out of trouble."

Clint walked back up the stairs to his room, wondering why Robinson had given up so easily. One glass of brandy and he said good night. It was hardly worth coming up to Clint's room and inviting him down to his office.

Unless . . .

He crept down the hall toward his door, his hand on his gun. Then he thought better of it and tried the doorknob of Crapface's door. It turned. He opened the door and entered.

"What the fuck—" Crapface said. He was lying on his back in bed, but had obviously not been asleep. "What's goin' on?"

"Did you hear anyone outside my room?"

"A little while ago," Crapface said, "somebody was knockin'."

"No, not then. Just now."

"Not before you. Why?"

Clint told Crapface about Sam Robinson's visit to his room, and his accompanying the man down to his office.

"Why'd you go?"

"I was curious, but now I'm thinking maybe it was a diversion."

"To get somebody into your room?"

"Yes."

"Why?"

"I don't know," Clint said. "To get the drop on me. Kill me?"

"If both sides want to recruit you, why would anyone from either side wanna kill you?"

Clint shrugged.

"I can see a reason for John Cross to want to kill me."

"What?"

"A girl."

"What girl have you gotten into trouble with now, Clint?"

"None . . . yet. But the colonel's daughter, Joyce, she's . . ."

"What?"

"Interested."

"Interested, or interesting?"

"Both."

"You better watch out, Clint. Be careful."

"That's what I'm doing," Clint said. "Can you get up?"

"Why?"

"I want you to lock this door after I go out."

Crapface tried to sit up, but couldn't.

"Never mind," Clint said. "I'll take your key and lock it myself."

"I'll be locked in."

"You're not going anywhere," Clint said, taking the key from a nearby table. "Where's your rifle?"

Crapface reached down to the floor and lifted it up.

"Good. Keep it handy."

"Now you think somebody's gonna try to kill me?" Crapface asked.

"Don't you remember?" Clint asked. "Somebody already tried."

When he was in the hall, he locked Crapface's door and pocketed the key. Then he turned his attention to his own door. For all intents and purposes, it looked just as he'd left it. With Robinson alongside him, he had taken no precautions, so he didn't know if anyone was waiting inside or not.

There was only one way to find out.

He drew his gun, put his own key in the door, and turned it.

TWENTY-THREE

Clint had found women in his room before.

He'd found naked women in his room before.

He'd even found dead women in his room before.

He'd never found a Joyce Woods in his room before.

Sitting on his bed, fully clothed, she was more desirable than many of the nude women he'd found in his bed.

He'd had an idea that a woman might come to his room, but he thought it would be the girl from the saloon again, pretty Penny.

"Are you disappointed you have nobody to shoot?" she asked.

"I would ask you if your father knows you're here, or Cross, but in both cases I hope the answer is no."

"Oh, it's no," she said. "Don't worry. I wouldn't want my father to find me here. He still thinks I'm his virginal little daughter."

"And you're not?"

"Little?"

"Virginal?"

"Oh, no," she said. She was still wearing the same dress she'd had on at dinner, but she had pulled the hem up to show him her legs, which she had crossed. She was also wearing sexy dark stockings.

He walked to the bedpost, holstered the gun, then removed the holster and hung it there.

"What about Cross?" he asked.

"What about him?"

"Does he think you're a virgin?" he asked. "Or does he know different?"

She smiled, a wide, lovely smile that lit up the entire room.

"Are you asking me if John is my lover?"

"I just want to know what I'm dealing with," he said, "before I take off all my clothes and jump on you."

She looked startled, then laughed.

"You're planning on jumping on me?"

"Oh, yes," Clint said, "but not if Cross is going to come through the door with a gun."

"He's not."

"Are you sure?"

"Positive."

"How can you be positive?" He sat on the bed and began to remove his boots.

"Well, for one thing, he's not my lover. He wishes he was, but he's not."

"Good."

She began to roll her black stockings down her legs as she spoke.

"Second, I made sure I wasn't followed here. He thinks I'm safe in my own bed."

Clint's boots and socks hit the floor, and he started on his shirt.

"How much do you know about him?" he asked.

"He's a killer," she said, "who my father is going to try to turn into a lawman."

"What do you know about Sam Robinson?"

"He's a hotel owner who's going to try to turn himself into a lawman."

"Do you think either can do the job?"

"Cross can."

"Your father wants you to marry him, you know."

"Oh, I know," she said. She loosened her dress, took the top in both of her hands, preparing to pull it down, but first she turned to him and said, "I don't have any intention of becoming the wife of a killer, or a sheriff."

She pulled the dress down and her bare breasts spilled out.

Outside the hotel John Cross watched the lights in the rooms. He didn't know for sure what Joyce Woods was doing in the hotel. He had an idea, but he was hoping he was wrong.

There were actually only two reasons he could think of. One was to see his opponent, Sam Robinson, only he couldn't imagine what she would want with him. He was, after all, not only Cross's opponent for the position of sheriff, but also her father's opponent for control of the town.

The other person she could be there to see was Clint Adams. The looks the two had been giving each other at dinner had not escaped Cross.

He was not foolish enough to think that Joyce was still a virgin. He left that kind of blind stupidity to her father. And even if she was in the hotel with Clint Adams, Cross still planned on marrying her. But if Clint Adams *was* putting his hands on her, the future sheriff of Woodsdale was going to make sure he paid.

John Cross was not impressed with the reputation of the Gunsmith.

TWENTY-FOUR

As her breasts spilled from her dress, Clint reached out and caught them. They were heavy in his hands, just the way he liked them. Warm, smooth, solid, large nipples, wide aureoles. Yes, exactly how he like them.

Joyce ran her hands over his chest as well. They sat there, both naked to the waist, and did some exploring. He bent, lifted her breasts to his mouth, and tongued her nipples awhile before sucking them into his mouth. He rolled them between his lips, flicked them with his tongue, and then nibbled them.

She gasped, reached for his head, held him there for what seemed like a long time, and then brought his lips up so she could kiss him. Her mouth was hot, avid, and sweet. They kissed for a long time, so that when they parted, her lips were slightly swollen. Her nipples were also sore, but it was a good soreness.

Abruptly, she reached for his belt and started to undo it. He stood, pulled her to her feet, and yanked her dress the rest of the way to the floor. She stepped out of it, kicked it away, and stood there naked. There was nothing shy or awkward in her stance. In fact, she stood with her hands on her hips, breasts thrust out, while he removed his pants.

"I could feel your eyes on me all through dessert," she told him.

"You're a beautiful woman."

She looked down at his swollen penis.

"And you're a beautiful man."

They moved together and, skin to skin, kissed again for a long time. His penis was trapped between them, rubbing up against her belly, smooth flesh against smooth flesh.

He slid his hands down the smooth line of her back to her buttocks, grabbed them, and turned her around. He squeezed her buttocks, which were taut, the skin resilient. He bit her and she gasped, then he kissed both cheeks, licked the crevice between them.

Her legs went weak just as he moved her to the bed. They fell on it again, still trapped in a tight, hot embrace. Once on the bed, they began to crawl all over each other.

Finally, he ended up on top. He kissed her long neck, worked his way down to her breasts, where he spent a long time on her nipples. He loved nipples. The thing about them was most women had beautiful nipples, no matter what size their breasts were. But he preferred his nipples attached to large, heavy breasts, and hers certainly qualified.

Slowly, he worked his way down her body until his face was nestled in the warm place between her thighs. She moaned and cried out as he eagerly tasted her. She grew so wet she began to soak the sheet beneath them. The smell of her was sharp and sweet at the same time. He lapped at her eagerly, because as sweet as she smelled, she tasted even sweeter.

He used his mouth on her until she was on the verge of screaming, and then he mounted and entered her. She wrapped her long legs around him and laughed with delight as he took her hard and fast . . .

Later, she used her hands and mouth on him, proving that she was no virgin. She sucked him until he couldn't take it any longer, and he exploded, then slumped in exhaustion. She nestled her head onto his shoulder, also exhausted, and they drifted off to sleep together . . .

When they awoke, they made love one more time tenderly, and then he asked, "Are you staying all night?"

"I wish I could, but I can't," she said with a sigh. "My father will wonder where I am."

"Won't he think you're with Cross?"

She laughed and said, "Probably."

"Then what's the difference?" he said. "It's pretty late anyway."

She snuggled up against him and said, "You're probably right."

"But what about Cross?" Clint asked.

She reached beneath the sheet, took hold of his penis, and said. "I can handle John Cross."

He didn't doubt it.

When Joyce Woods didn't come out of the hotel by the time the saloons closed, John Cross decided to pack it in. He had no doubt that she was with Clint Adams, so Adams had now moved himself to the top of the list.

A list he didn't want to be on at all.

TWENTY-FIVE

In the morning they woke each other energetically, and then she got dressed.

"We can't have breakfast together," Joyce said. "I'll have to sneak back into the house so I can change these clothes."

"That's all right," Clint said. "I'll console myself with a huge breakfast."

"A large meal will make up for not having me as a breakfast companion?"

"Just barely," he said.

She stuck her tongue out at him. They had talked very little during the night, and yet she realized she felt very close to him. She didn't know why, but she didn't object to the feeling anyway.

"Where can I get a good steak-and-egg breakfast?" he asked her.

"Just walk down the street and follow your nose," she said.

She walked to the bed and kissed him, her hands on his bare chest.

"You won't be leaving town today, will you?" she asked.

"I doubt my friend will be ready to ride," Clint said. "No, we'll be here at least another day."

"Good," she said. "I'll see you later."

Before he could say anything, she hurried from the room.

He slept another hour, then awoke, washed, and got dressed. His shirt was grimy, which reminded him of his friend. He went across the hall, knocked, and used the key to enter Crapface's room.

"It's about time," the buffalo hunter said. "I've been awake for hours, and starving."

"Sorry," Clint said, "I've been busy."

"Yeah, I heard."

"From across the hall?"

"The walls are very thin," Crapface said. "Who was it? Girl from the saloon?"

"Joyce Woods."

"The colonel's daughter?"

"Yes," Clint said. "As it turns out, she's very aggressive."

"You and aggressive women," Crapface said. "A great match."

"When they brought you the food yesterday, did they bring anything else?"

"Yeah, some packages wrapped in brown paper. Over there."

Clint found them and tore them open.

"What is it?" Crapface asked.

"Clean shirts."

"Must be for you."

"Yes."

Clint took off his grimy shirt and donned the new one. It was crisp and clean. He tossed the other one into a corner.

"What's wrong with that one?"

"Dirty."

"Not hardly," Crapface said. "It looked okay to me. Better than mine."

"You can have it."

"And you can take those others."

"I'll pick them up later," Clint said as he walked to the door. "When I bring back some breakfast for you."

"And when will that be?"

"Soon."

Clint opened the door and stepped into the hall.

"You're not gonna run into another girl, are you?" Crapface asked.

Clint reached for the door to close it and said, "Not until I bring you your food."

"Steak and eggs!" Crapface yelled.

"What else?" Clint replied with a shrug, and pulled the door shut.

Clint saw what Joyce had meant by following his nose. There were quite a few tents that were serving food. He stopped at a couple, found them cramped and crowded, then finally went into the third, where there were some empty seats.

He sat down and a waiter came over.

"Help ya?"

"Steak and eggs," Clint said. "When I'm done, I'll need another to take with me."

"Yes, sir."

"And coffee, strong."

"Comin' up."

Clint had seated himself so he could see the front flap of the tent. He saw John Cross as soon as he entered. Cross walked directly to him, so he knew the man had known he was there.

"Can I join you?" he asked.

"I thought you'd be eating breakfast with the colonel," Clint said.

"That meal was for your benefit," Cross said. "The colonel usually eats at home."

"Then have a seat. I've got coffee coming."

He saw the waiter coming toward them, so he held up two fingers. The waiter nodded, and when he arrived, he had a pot of coffee and two mugs. He poured the two mugs full, and then waited for Cross to order.

"Ham and eggs."

"Yes, sir."

Cross looked at Clint, who scanned the room, drank from his mug, then finally turned his attention to the man in front of him.

"What can I do for you, Mr. Cross?"

"Sheriff Cross."

"Not yet," Clint said. "There still has to be an election, doesn't there?"

"It's a formality."

"That's what the colonel told you, right? I don't think Sam Robinson thinks so."

"You saw Robinson?"

"We had a talk."

"What about?" Cross asked. "What did Robinson want from you?"

"The same thing the colonel wanted."

"And what did you tell him?"

"Same thing I told the colonel . . . no."

Cross stared at Clint some more, then asked, "Is that what you told Joyce?"

"What's that?"

"Joyce Woods," Cross said. "When she came to your room last night, did you tell her no?"

Clint thought about it for a moment, then said, "First of all, I'm not saying she came to my room last night. It's not something a gentleman discusses. And second, why don't you ask her?"

"I will," Cross said, "don't worry."

The waiter came with their breakfast, set their plates down in front of them.

"I'm hungry," Cross said.

"Me, too."

"I don't like to talk while I eat."

"Me neither."

They started to eat.

TWENTY-SIX

"You mind talking over coffee?" Clint asked when they had finished their breakfast.

"About what?" Cross asked.

"I don't know," Clint said. "You came here looking for me, right?"

"No," Cross said. "I followed you from your hotel."

"I know," Clint said. "And badly, too."

"Believe me," Cross said, "if I didn't want you to see me, you wouldn't have."

"Cross," Clint said, "I have half a mug of coffee left. You have that much time to get to the point."

"I don't want you around," Cross said. "I don't need your help. If you get in my way, I'll kill you. Is that to the point enough?"

"Does your boss know you feel this way?"

"Don't worry, I'll tell him. I'm tellin' you first," Cross said.

Clint finished his coffee and put the mug down. Then, true to his word, he stood up and walked out.

Conversation over.

Clint had to wait across the street for Cross to leave before he could go back in and pick up Crapface's breakfast. He couldn't go back in while Cross was still there, not after his very deliberate exit.

He opened Crapface's door with his key and entered the room.

"It's about time," his friend said. "I'm starved!"

"Sorry," Clint said. "I had a guest at breakfast, and got held up."

He handed Crapface the tray bearing a plate of steak and eggs, a knife and a fork.

"No beer? I need something to wash this down with."

"Sorry, I couldn't carry coffee back."

"Who was your guest?" Crapface asked, cutting into his meat.

"John Cross."

"The would-be sheriff?"

"That's the one."

"What did he want?"

"Just to tell me he'd kill me if I got in his way."

"And how would you get in his way?"

"Maybe by staying in town and siding with his opponent," Clint said. "Or taking the colonel's offer. But I think he was really talking about the colonel's daughter."

"Oh, Jeez—" Crapface said, making a pained face.

"He said he knew she came to my room last night."

"And what did you say?"

"I didn't address it," Clint said. "Let him talk to her if he has a problem."

"Why don't you talk you her," Crapface suggested, "and tell her to stay away from you. She's only trouble, Clint."

"Yeah," Clint said, "but wrapped up in such a pretty package."

Crapface chewed and shook his head, gestured with his knife.

"You're gonna get yerself killed because of a woman, mark my words."

"We all have to die sometime."

"Yeah, well, I'd just as soon be trampled by a herd of buffalo—and my chances of that are gettin' slimmer and slimmer. If we don't get up to the panhandle, the last of those buffalo are gonna be dead."

"I'm going to get the doctor to come and have a look at you," Clint said. "If he says it's okay, we'll leave tomorrow morning."

"How about right now?"

"Tomorrow morning, Tyrone."

"Jesus," Crapface said, looking both pained and aggrieved, "don't go callin' me by my proper name. I hate it!"

TWENTY-SEVEN

Clint found the doctor with a patient, a boy who had broken his arm and his very concerned and tired-looking mother.

"I need time to treat this boy's arm," the doctor said to Clint.

"Doctor, will he be all right?" the mother asked.

"He'll be fine, Mrs. Lance. Come in with me, you can be with him while I treat him."

Clint waited for the sawbones to treat the damaged limb, then walked with him back to the hotel.

"Is that pretty much the type of thing you handle?" Clint asked him. "Or are gunshot wounds more the normal thing?"

"This is pretty much a normal boomtown, Mr. Adams," the doctor said. "We get all kinds of injuries here—broken arms and legs, gunshot wounds, folks run down by buckboards, injuries from fights—and that's not even mentioning women who give birth."

"Sounds like you're busy."

"Most days."

"I appreciate you taking the time to check on Crapface."

"I've been meaning to ask, is that really his name?" the doctor asked.

"Pretty much what everybody calls him," Clint explained.

"Why would he stand for that?"

"Because it's also what he calls himself."

"Why would he do that?"

"Because his real name's Tyrone."

"Oh."

Clint used the key to unlock the door. The doctor watched, frowning.

"Just being safe," he told the doctor. "Crapface isn't exactly spry at the moment. We don't want anyone surprising him."

They entered and Crapface looked up at them from the bed.

"Hey, Doc!" he said anxiously. "Take a look at my shoulder and let this fella know I can ride okay, won't ya?"

"I'll take a look, Mr. Jones," the doctor said, "but I can't promise anything."

The doctor unbuttoned Crapface's new long johns, which Clint was seeing for the first time. Then he unbandaged the wound so he could examine it, probe it a bit with his fingers. Crapface tried not to, but he winced and caught his breath.

"Hurt?" the doctor asked.

"Naw," Crapface lied.

The doctor cleaned the wound and then applied a fresh bandage.

"So?" Crapface asked. "Whataya say, Doc? Can I ride out?"

"Not yet, I'm afraid," the doctor said. "If you try, you'll likely tear your stitches and start to bleed. You need another day or two."

"Aw, Jesus," Crapface said. "I can't stay in this bed for another two days."

"Well," the doctor said, "you could go outside, sit in a chair in front of the hotel. Get some air."

"That's all?" Crapface asked. "Sit in a chair?"

"It's better than lying on that bed," Clint pointed out, "isn't it?"

Crapface crossed his arms, winced, and said, "Maybe you're right."

"I'll stop in again tomorrow," the doctor promised. "As soon as I see that those stitches won't come apart, I'll give you the go-ahead."

Begrudgingly, Crapface said, "Thanks, Doc."

Clint nodded to the doctor, who left.

"Want me to help you outside?" Clint asked.

"I guess so," Crapface said. "I'll need my boots."

Clint looked over at Crapface's worn boots in the corner of the room, with his soiled socks lying on top of them.

"It's a good thing we're such good friends," he said with a sigh.

Out in front of the hotel Clint found two wooden chairs and set them down on the boardwalk. Then he sat Crapface down in one of them, and sat himself down in the other one. Crapface was wearing the grimy shirt Clint had discarded, and his own worn trousers and boots. He had left the skins in the room.

"How's that?" Clint asked. "Better?"

"Some," Crapface said reluctantly. "At least I'm gettin' some fresh air on my face."

Crapface took a deep breath then stared out at the muddy streets and motley collection of tents. The only other buildings were behind them, so he couldn't see them.

"Not much to look at," he said.

"Most towns aren't when they start out," Clint said.

"And some of them don't get very far," Crapface said. "I've seen towns boom, and then die."

"I know," Clint said. "Leadville, Dodge, some of them lasted longer than others."

"This one may not last long at all," Crapface said. "This colonel sounds a little too . . . out for himself."

"I agree," Clint said.

"And Cross, he's got his own interests."

"Maybe that other town, Hugoton, has got people who are working together."

"I wonder if we'll have to pass by that one to get to the panhandle," Crapface said. "And I do mean pass by. I don't wanna make any more stops."

"I agree with that," Clint said. "No more unscheduled stops."

TWENTY-EIGHT

Colonel Woods looked up as John Cross entered his office. They were in Woods's house, which was the first building the colonel had erected when he came to "Woodsdale." After that came the hotel.

"Where've you been?" the colonel asked.

"Out."

"Doing what?"

Cross sat down across from his boss.

"Marking my territory, I guess."

"What do you mean?" the colonel asked. "Were you in a pissing contest?"

"I guess you could call it that."

Woods laughed, sat back from his paperwork.

"With who?"

"Clint Adams."

Now Woods guffawed, to the point of choking.

"You've got more *cojones* than even I gave you credit

for," he said. "What the hell were you doing putting yours up against the Gunsmith?"

"Well, for one thing, we don't need him."

"And you told him so?"

"That's right."

"And why don't we need him?"

"Because I'm gonna be sheriff, and that's all we need," Cross said.

"You don't think the election would go smoother for you with him on your ticket as your deputy?"

"No."

"Well," Woods said, "what if I told you that I do think you'd do better with him? What if I said I need him? What then?"

"Then I'd say get yourself another boy," Cross said. He started to get up.

"Okay, wait a minute," the colonel said. "Don't be in such a rush."

Cross settled back into his chair.

"How about a brandy?"

Cross frowned. Woods usually didn't offer him a drink. Not after their first meeting anyway.

Woods poured two glasses of brandy and handed one to Cross.

"All right," he said, sitting behind his desk again, "tell me what this is really about."

Cross maintained a stubborn silence.

"It's Joyce, isn't it?"

"What?"

Woods laughed.

"Come on, Cross," he said. "I saw the looks they were giving each other at the table last night. You saw them, too."

Cross sat forward in his chair.

"She's supposed to marry me, not mess with some saddle tramp who's passin' through."

"I'd hardly call the Gunsmith a saddle tramp."

"You're impressed with his reputation."

"And you're not."

"No."

"Don't tell me you threatened to kill him?"

"Only if he got in my way."

Woods shook his head.

"Did you know he talked to Robinson?"

"I didn't know," Woods said, "but he's staying in Sam's hotel, so that's no surprise."

"Robinson tried to recruit him."

"And?"

"He told him no, like he told you."

"Well, then you don't have any problems, do you?" Woods asked. "As soon as his friend heals, they'll be on their way."

"Can't be too soon for me."

"Of course," Woods said, "if you want to ensure your election—and your reputation . . ."

"What are you driving at?"

"You and the Gunsmith, in the street."

"I don't get it," Cross said. "Now you want me to kill him?"

"I'm just thinking that maybe he can do us more good dead than alive."

"How so?"

"You've got to be smarter, Cross," Woods said. "Who do you think this town, this county, would vote in as their sheriff—Sam Robinson, or the man who killed the famous Gunsmith?"

"I see your point."

"There's only one thing wrong with that."

"What?"

"Can you do it?"

"I can do it," Cross said. "You just tell me where and when."

"I'll work that out," Woods said. "Don't you worry about it."

TWENTY-NINE

Joyce Woods was standing outside her father's office, listening to the conversation between him and John Cross. She hurried away before Cross left, so he wouldn't catch her. Now in her room, she was wondering what she should do. Confront her father, tell him that she'd heard him and Cross planning murder? Or tell Clint Adams, which would mean betraying her father?

Maybe the man to talk to was Cross. That was it. He loved her, wanted to marry him. Maybe if she agreed to that, he'd forget about the plot to kill Clint Adams. And she wasn't only trying to save Clint's life, but her father's life and reputation as well. If it ever came out, he'd be ruined. That would kill him.

She decided to go and see Cross right away, see if she could sway him. If he loved her enough, wanted her enough, it should be easy.

She pulled on a shawl and hurried down the stairs, but before she could go out the front door, she heard her father's voice.

"Where are you off to?"

She stopped short and turned to face him.

"I'm just . . . going out."

"Joyce," he said, "this is not the kind of place for you to be walking around alone. It's dangerous out there. Somebody could get killed."

"I know that, Father. I was just . . . going to see John."

"Cross? About what?"

"I . . . just want to talk to him."

"Well, he was just here," Woods said. "If I'd known you wanted to talk to him, I would have called you down."

"That's all right," she said. "I want to talk to him alone."

"Is this about . . . well, the two of you?"

"Yes," she said, "that's what it's about."

"Joyce," Woods said, "if I were you, I wouldn't do anything to spoil the plan now."

"The plan?"

"For you and John to marry," he said. "It's not easy for a girl to find a man who actually wants to get married these days."

"I know that, too, Father."

"And if I was you," her father said, "I'd stay away from that Gunsmith fellow."

"Really?" She turned to face him. "Stay away from him?"

"Now, now," he said, taking her by the shoulders, "don't take an attitude with me, honey. I'm just trying to do what's best for everyone."

"Everyone?"

"Yes," he said, "you, me, John Cross, the town, the county."

"What about Clint Adams?" she asked. "What's best for him?"

"I don't know," he said. "I think that's up to him to worry about."

"That's right," she said. "You have enough to think about, don't you?"

She turned and put her hand on the doorknob.

"Joyce! You're not still going out, are you?" he asked, alarmed.

"I told you, Father," she said. "I want to talk to John, and I want to talk to him now!"

"You headstrong girl—" he started, but she opened the door and went out.

Headstrong, he thought, just like her mother used to be.

She found Cross as he was coming out of one of the saloon tents.

"Joyce," he said, "what are you doing on the street? This is no place for you to be walking around alone. It's too dangerous."

"That's what Father keeps telling me."

"Well, he's right."

"You think he's right about everything, don't you?" she asked.

"No," he said, "not everything. Come on, I'll walk you home."

"No," she said. "Take me someplace where we can talk . . . alone."

"All right," he said. "We'll go and have some coffee. Come on. We can get a table in a corner, where nobody can hear us."

He took her by the elbow and led her away from the saloon.

THIRTY

"Hey," Crapface said, "ain't that your girl?"

"Huh? Where?"

"Straight ahead."

They had been sitting there over an hour. They could see right down the street, but not as far as the saloon tents.

"That's Miss Woods, ain't it?" Crapface asked. "With the soon-to-be Sheriff Cross?"

"The want-to-be Sheriff Cross, and yes, that's her."

"I wonder where they're goin'," Crapface asked. "And what they're doin'."

"Looks to me like they're going to get something to eat."

As Joyce and Cross entered a tent, Clint knew that it was one that served food.

"Guess they're having a late breakfast," he commented.

"Or an early lunch," Crapface said. "Do you want to go and find out?"

"Not really," Clint said. "I've had my conversation with Mr. Cross."

"And a long conversation with Miss Woods," Crapface reminded him. "Don't forget that."

"How could I?"

They sat silently for a while, and then Crapface asked, "Think they're talkin' about us?"

"Why would they?" Clint asked.

"I dunno," Crapface said. "What else would there be to talk about in this town?"

"There must be a lot," Clint said.

But he had to admit, he also wondered if he was a subject of conversation between the two people. After all, they'd both spent time with him recently. Under very different circumstances.

Cross and Joyce got a table in the rear of the tent. There were only a few other people there, and they were able to speak without being overheard.

They ordered coffee, then waited quietly until their server had poured it and left.

"What can I do for you, Joyce?" Cross asked when they were alone.

She had debated with herself how to approach this, and she decided just to go straight ahead.

"I heard you and my father talking this morning."

"You did?"

She nodded.

"Do you often eavesdrop on your father?"

"Never," she said, "but I did today."

"And what do you think you heard?"

"I heard you and him talking about killing Clint Adams."

"No," Cross said, "you must have heard wrong."

"Really?" she asked. "Then what *were* you talking about?"

"How to get Adams to help us."

"By killing him?" she asked. "And making a name for yourself?"

He reached across the table for her hand. She wanted to pull away but decided not to.

"You can't go around saying things like this, Joyce," he said. "For one thing, you'll get your father in trouble."

"And you?"

"Yes, and me."

"Then you won't kill Clin—Mr. Adams?"

"No, of course not."

"Not even if my father tells you to?"

"I don't think he'd do that, but no . . . not if you don't want me to."

"I don't."

Now he took her hand in both of his.

"But who is your concern for?" he asked. "Adams, or me?"

"Why, you, of course, John."

"Joyce, you know your father expects us to marry, don't you?"

"I do."

"You'll be the sheriff's wife."

"Yes."

"But I won't be the sheriff forever," he said. "I expect to move up."

"I know you will, John."

"I had better walk you home now."

He paid the bill and they stepped outside. She looked up

the street and saw the hotel, with two men sitting out front. She recognized Clint.

She knew what her father and Cross had talked about, but she let Cross think that he had persuaded her she had heard wrong.

In order to get to her home, they were going to have to walk past the hotel. She took his arm, and they headed that way.

Cross saw Clint sitting in front of the hotel with his friend. He intended to walk Joyce right by them. Joyce may have thought she'd persuaded him not to kill Clint Adams, but that was not the case. Now he had to go to her father and they had to figure out what to do with her before they killed him. She might not turn her father in for murder, but she could very well turn him in. After all, he wasn't family. Not yet anyway.

"They're comin' this way," Crapface said.

"I see them."

"Don't say nothin'."

"That would be rude."

"Okay, then don't say nothin' unless one of them does," Crapface said. "And don't say nothin' that'll make 'em mad."

"Yeah, okay," Clint said. "That I can do."

They watched the two people walking toward them, wondering if they were coming to the hotel, or if they were going to pass it by.

THIRTY-ONE

As they approached, Clint noticed that Joyce was taking great pains not to look his way. He thought her effort was wasted. He was sure that Cross knew about them.

It seemed as if they were going to pass the hotel by, probably on the way to her father's house, but suddenly Cross changed direction. In moments they were standing right in front of where Clint and Crapface were seated.

"Mr. Adams," Cross said, "I'm sure you remember Miss Woods?"

"Yes, I do," Clint said. "Hello, Joyce."

"Mr. Adams," she said, keeping up her hopeless pretext.

"And your injured friend," Cross said. "I've forgotten his name."

"Jones," Clint said, "this is Tyrone Jones."

"How are you feeling, Mr. Jones?" Cross asked.

"Better," Crapface said, "much better."

"That's good," Cross said. "Then you'll be on your way soon."

"Not soon enough."

Cross touched the brim of his hat and they moved on. Joyce did not look back.

"Not soon enough?" Clint said to Crapface. "I thought you said not to say anything that might make them mad."

"Couldn't help it," Crapface said. "I wanna get out of this town before you have to kill somebody else, or somebody kills you."

"I wouldn't like that either."

"That man," Crapface said, "wants to kill you."

"I know."

"And if we stay here, he'll try it."

"I know."

"And either he'll kill you, or you'll kill him."

"Jesus, Crapface," Clint said. "I get it."

"Just makin' sure," the buffalo hunter said. "Hey, why don't we go get us a couple of beers?"

"You're not going anywhere," Clint said. "But a beer sounds good. I'll go get them and bring them back."

"Okay," Crapface said, "but make it fast so they don't get warm."

Clint stood up and said, "I'll be back as fast as I can."

"I'll be right here."

"You better be."

Clint walked to the saloon he and Crapface had been in before. Might as well stay with what he knew.

He went to the bar, where Brent was tending.

"Well, I thought maybe you were gone."

"Not 'til my friend heals," Clint said.

"Where is he?"

"Over at the hotel. I need two beers to take over there."

"I gotta put 'em in pails."

"That's okay."

"Be right back."

While he was waiting, Penny came walking up to him.

"Well, where have you been?" she asked, bumping him with her hip.

"My friend had an accident," he said. "I've been taking care of him."

"That's a good friend," she said. "But I thought you were gonna be my friend."

"I am your friend," he said. "I thought I proved that already."

"I think I'm gonna need a bit more proof before we're done," she said.

She smiled, went off to do her job.

Brent returned with two pails of beer. Clint paid him and left.

"That *was* fast," Crapface said.

Clint handed him one pail, then sat down with the other one.

"That's good," Crapface said after a long drink.

"Make it last," Clint said. "I'm not going back again."

"Trouble?"

"Another girl."

"Oh, the blond saloon girl? She ain't gonna be any trouble."

"There would be if she came to my room the same time as Joyce."

"That one better not come to your room," Crapface said. "Not anymore."

Clint drank some beer and said, "We'll have to wait and see."

THIRTY-TWO

"Back so soon?" Woods asked as Cross entered.

Cross looked out into the hall, then pulled the door closed behind him.

"What's going on?" Woods asked.

"She heard us talking before."

"Who did?"

"Joyce!"

Woods frowned.

"What did she hear?"

Cross paced.

"She heard us talking about killing the Gunsmith," he said.

"She told you this?"

"Yes."

"Why didn't she come to me?"

"You'll have to ask her that."

"What did she say to you?"

"She asked me not to kill him."

"Why?"

"Because doing it would get you and me into trouble."

"And you believe her? I mean, that's her reason?" Woods asked.

"Why else?"

"Maybe she's in love with him."

"She hardly knows him."

"You said she was with him last night."

"So what?" Cross asked. "She's not going to fall in love with him after one night. We're still going to get married."

"You think so?"

"We agreed."

Cross sat back in his chair.

"I'll talk to her."

"I already did," he said. "She agreed not to tell anyone."

"I'll talk to her anyway."

"Do you want me to get her?"

"No," Woods said. "Don't worry about it. I'll speak with her."

"All right," Cross said. "Let me know what happens when you talk to her."

"Don't worry," Woods said. "She won't say a word. We're still on track. Take your first opportunity to kill Adams. Get some help if you have to, but make it look like a fair fight."

After Cross left, Woods sat at his desk for a very long time, going over his options.

He could forget about using Clint Adams, and just let him leave town.

He could ship Joyce back East, keep her out of the way so she wouldn't be a problem. But in the East or here, she could still tell someone what he was planning.

He could have his own daughter killed.

Would Cross do it? No. He was in love with her. Cross thought he was a killer, but he had limits—not many, but refusing to kill the woman he loved was one of them.

If Woods decided to kill Joyce, he'd need somebody with no limits at all.

But that was ridiculous.

He was an ambitious man, saw Woodsdale and this new county as a way to further his own political ambitions, but even he wouldn't sacrifice his own child.

Would he?

Joyce sat in her room, wondering what was going on downstairs. Wondering if she'd made a mistake. Maybe she should have gone to her father first.

She went to her window and looked out, saw John Cross waking away. What had he told her father? And what had her father told him?

What was going to happen?

THIRTY-THREE

"Okay," Clint said.

"Okay, what?" Crapface asked.

"Okay, I've had enough of just sitting here."

"So have I."

"Yeah, well, the difference is, I can leave and you can't."
Clint stood up.

"I don't want to sit here alone."

"Your only other choice is to go back to your room," Clint
said.

"Jesus, that ain't much of a choice."

"I'm going to see if I can find out what's going on around
here, for real."

"Wait, wait," Crapface said. "You can't leave me here
without my rifle."

"You want to go back to your room and get it?" Clint
asked.

"No, I want you to go to my room and get it, bring it to

me here. I'll stay out here awhile longer, but not without my Sharps."

"Okay," Clint said, pointing his finger, "but you better be here when I get back."

"I'll be here."

"If you're not, I'll get a set of chains from the sheriff and chain you to your bed."

"Okay, okay," Crapface said, "but remember, he's the almost sheriff."

Clint hurried up to Crapface's room, grabbed his Sharps and some rounds, and took them back downstairs. He was almost surprised to find Crapface still sitting there.

"What?" his friend said. "I tol' you I'd stay here, didn't I? Gimme."

He put his hand out and Clint placed the Sharps in it.

"Rounds?"

Clint handed over six rounds. Crapface put them in his pocket.

"Okay," he said, "I'm ready."

"For what?"

"With Baby in my hands," Crapface said, "anything."

"I forgot you call that thing Baby."

"Just a pet name," Crapface said. "You never named your gun?"

"Yeah," Clint said, "it's call Gun." He pointed again. "Stay here, or in your room."

"Gotcha."

Crapface placed his Sharps over his legs.

Clint walked into the center of Woodsdale, where activity was at its height. It was getting on to late afternoon. There was still some construction going on, but soon those workers would be done for the day and would flock into the saloons. Or maybe they'd line up to sign their names.

Clint decided to go into the saloon before it got crowded, and see how much information he could get from Brent, Penny, and some of the others who worked there.

He entered and approached the bar.

John Cross saw Clint Adams go into the saloon. He assumed that Joyce Woods was still at her father's house, where he had left her. So this might turn out to be his best chance to kill Adams, since Colonel Woods said they were still on track to carry out their plans.

He crossed the street to enter the saloon.

THIRTY-FOUR

"What kind of information are you lookin' for?" Brent, the bartender, asked after he'd served Clint a cold beer. He leaned on the bar to listen.

"Colonel Woods," Clint said.

"What about him?"

"What's he really after around here?"

"Well," Brent said, "he's already got a town named after him, but somehow I don't think he's gonna stop there."

"How do you mean?"

"If you want specifics, I got none," Brent said. "All I know is what I hear from men who come in here. Some folks have their doubts about the colonel. They think he ain't exactly out for the good of the town in this fight with Hugoton."

"What about Cross?"

Brent shrugged.

"He's pretty much the colonel's man," Brent said. "He'll

do what the old man wants him to do—especially if it means he gets to be the sheriff, and marry the colonel's daughter."

"And what about Sam Robinson?"

"What about him?"

"What kind of a sheriff would he make?" Clint asked him.

"I don't know what kind of sheriff either of them would make," Brent said. "I don't know either man except to serve them drinks, and to hear what other folks say about them."

"So you've heard a lot about them."

"That may be, but what I've heard I can't swear is true."

"Tell me anyway."

"I've heard people say that Cross would make a better lawman," Brent answered, "and Robinson a better politician."

"And what's needed around here right now?" Clint asked.

"In the early days of this town, probably a lawman," Brent said. "But if John Cross becomes the sheriff, Colonel Woods will still be around, and he's definitely a politician."

"So by voting Cross in," Clint said, "you'll get two for one."

"I suppose so."

Clint finished his beer and set the empty mug down on the bar. Brent stood up straight.

"Another one?"

"Why not?"

He looked around while the bartender got him another beer.

"Where's Penny?" he asked when the bartender came back.

"Off working somewhere."

"Working?"

Brent gave Clint a knowing look.

"She doesn't only serve drinks," he said, "if you know what I mean."

Clint understood.

"In fact, I think she's over at the hotel," Brent added.

"The hotel?"

"With your friend."

"Crapface?" Clint asked.

Brent shook his head.

"Robinson."

THIRTY-FIVE

Clint nursed his second beer. He figured if he waited for Penny to come back, he might get some information from her about Robinson. The more information he had, the better informed he was, the better his decisions might be.

But what decisions did he have to make? He was only waiting for Crapface to heal so that they could ride out, and head for the Texas panhandle to hunt the last of the buffalo.

What did he care who ended up sheriff? Which town ended up the county seat? It didn't matter to him one way or the other. Except for the fact that he disliked both the colonel and would-be Sheriff Cross.

Maybe there was something he could do before he left to make their lives a little more difficult. Crapface wouldn't like it, but it would give Clint some pleasure.

He turned as a woman came through the tent flap. It was Penny.

* * *

Penny had disappeared for about half an hour, then returned, wearing a different dress, looking as if she was fresh from a bath—which she probably was.

She talked to some of the men in the place, gracing them with smiles as she passed, and joined Clint at the bar.

"A glass of whiskey, Brent," she said.

"Comin' up."

"It'll be on Mr. Adams here."

"My pleasure," Clint said.

"Were you waiting for me?" she asked. The smile she gave him was genuine, not the one she flashed at the men on the floor.

"Of course I was," he said. "I came in here looking for you."

"Liar," she said. "But I like it."

She touched his arm as Brent brought a shot glass of whiskey and set it in front of her.

"To your health," she said, lifting her glass.

"To your beauty," he said.

They drank.

"Why were you looking for me?" she asked.

"I wanted to see you," he said. "Do I need another reason?"

"Of course you do," she said. "You're a man, aren't you?"

"Well, all right," he said. "Let's sit down."

He took his beer and she left her empty glass on the bar. They went to a table in a corner. He wasn't very comfortable sitting anywhere in the saloon, since the walls were made of canvas, but he put that aside for the moment.

"I'll be leaving in a day or two," he said, "but I don't like what I'm leaving behind."

"Me? Then take me with you," she said. "Where are you going?"

"To hunt buffalo."

"Oh, pooh," she said. "I'll stay here. What is it you don't like about Woodsdale?"

"Well, for one thing, the man it's named after."

"The colonel?" she asked. "Well, that's nothing new. Nobody around here likes the colonel."

"I also don't like his choice for sheriff, John Cross."

"Why not? Seems to me he'll be a fine sheriff."

"I thought you'd be casting your vote for Sam Robinson," Clint said.

"Sam? But why—oh, I see," she said. "Brent told you where I was."

"He did."

"Well, just because Sam's a customer of mine doesn't mean I think he'd make a good sheriff."

"So you don't think he would?"

"Oh, I suppose he'd be all right," she said, "but he's a hotel owner. A politician. I don't even know if he can handle a gun."

"And Cross can."

"Yes."

"Is Cross one of your customers?"

"Oh, no," she said. "He hasn't used any of the girls. I think Mr. Cross is a one-woman man. I suppose he's to be admired for that."

"So you think he'll be elected?"

"With the colonel behind him? I don't think anyone has any doubt."

Clint sipped his beer.

"What are you going to do?" she asked. "You'll be leaving in a day or two."

"That's true," he said. "And I don't live here, so why should I care?"

"Why do you care?"

"Because he tried to buy me," he said.

THIRTY-SIX

Joyce Woods decided she had to get out of the house and warn Clint. It was what she should have done in the first place.

She left her room, made her way to the back of the house, and out the back door. She forgot her shawl, and was wearing only a simple cotton dress.

She was able to make her way quickly to the rear of the hotel, where she found the door unlocked. The desk clerk was dozing off as she entered the lobby.

"Hey!" she said, startling him.

"What can I do for ya, ma'am?"

"Is Clint Adams in his room?"

"No, ma'am," he said.

"Well, where is he?"

"Last I seen, he was sittin' out front with that other fella."

"His friend?"

"That's right."

She turned and rushed to the front door. She saw two

chairs, one empty, the other occupied by Clint's friend, who was sitting with his rifle across his legs.

"Where's Clint?" she asked.

Crapface looked up at her, a surprised look on his face.

"Where did you come from?" he asked.

"I cut through the hotel," she said. "I don't want my father to see me here."

"You're Miss Woods?"

"That's right. The desk clerk told me Clint was sitting out here."

"Well, he was out here, but he went into town," Crapface said.

"Alone?"

"There's only him and me," he said, "so yeah, he's alone. Why?"

She hesitated, then said, "I heard my father and John Cross talking about killing Clint."

"What for?"

"Well, he won't work for my father, so he doesn't want him working against him."

"He ain't gonna do neither, and I ain't gonna either," Crapface told her. "We're gonna be leavin' town soon."

"I'm afraid they'll kill him before that," she said. "He has to be warned."

"He ain't an easy man to kill, girl," Crapface said, "but I'll warn him."

"Now?"

"As soon as I see 'im."

She looked off down the street into town.

"Maybe I should go find him."

"I think you outta cut back through the hotel and get on back to your house, missy," Crapface said. "I'll get word to him."

"Are you sure?"

"I'm real sure."

She studied him critically.

"Are you sure you can walk?"

"I can walk," Crapface said. "And I can shoot. Don't you worry about Clint. Long as I'm around, nobody's killin' Clint Adams."

"I hope you're right."

"I am," he said. "Now you git before your pa starts lookin' for ya."

Reluctantly, she moved back into the hotel, and was gone.

She entered the house through the back door and made her way back to her room. Sitting on the bed, she clasped her hands together in her lap. After a few minutes she was thinking she couldn't just sit there and wait. She had to do something, no matter what Clint's friend said.

Something.

Colonel Woods heard Joyce come back into the house. He knew she had left, and he knew where she'd gone. She was warning Clint Adams. Well, that was okay with him. He was going to use that warning to his advantage.

Once he was sure she was back in her room, he strapped on his gun and left the house himself, through the front door.

Cross waited across the way from the saloon tent for Adams to come out, but as time started to pass, he wondered if Adams was in there for the rest of the day. Whiskey and girls were in there, and those things kept men like Clint Adams busy.

Maybe he had time to collect a little help.

THIRTY-SEVEN

Clint had a third beer, thought about bringing another one to Crapface, then decided to have another one himself.

Penny came over from time to time to hip-bump him as the place got busier and busier.

"Are you gettin' drunk?" she asked at one point.

"No," he said, "I'm just doing some thinking."

Later Brent came over and asked, "Want another one?"

"No."

The bartender looked at his half-filled mug and asked, "Freshen that one up?"

"No," Clint said, "I've got enough here to keep me thinking."

"Still about the colonel? And Cross?"

"Yup."

"Why would you even care?" Brent asked. "You ain't gonna live here."

"No, but some people are," Clint said. "They deserve good law."

"Good law?" Brent asked.

"That's right."

"Is there such a thing?"

Clint finished his beer and said, "There used to be."

Crapface went into the hotel lobby after Joyce had left, and he approached the desk.

"How do I get to the roof?"

John Cross could not recruit the wrong men for the job he had in mind. He couldn't afford to have this come back to haunt him after he was elected sheriff.

"So let me get this straight," one of the three men with him asked. They were in a small tent with a short bar and a few tables. The speaker was Al Carvey. The other two men were Ed Gentry and Lou Dale.

"If you were sheriff, we'd be deputies right now?" Carvey asked.

"That's right."

"So when you get to be sheriff," Dale asked, "we'll get to be deputies?"

"That depends."

"On what?"

"On how things go this time."

"And how do you want things to go, Mr. Cross?" Gentry asked.

"My way, Gentry," Cross said. "I always want things to go my way."

Gentry, Carvey, and Dale entered the saloon while Clint was working on his last beer. They spotted him immediately from Cross's description and approached the bar. Two them stood on Clint's left, and the other—Gentry—on his right.

Clint was aware that he was being hemmed in, looked at all three men. They pretended not to see him as they crowded him.

"Gents," Brent said, "there's plenty of room for everyone."

"Shut up and get us three beers," Carvey said.

Brent looked at Clint, who just nodded.

"Hey, mister," Carvey said, "how about givin' us some room?"

"Like the bartender said, friend, lots of room for everybody."

"Then why you takin' up my room . . . friend?" Gentry asked.

Clint knew what was going on. He moved a bit to his right to give Gentry room, thereby making contact with the other man, Carvey.

"Hey," Carvey said, "a little room here. You made me bump into my friend."

The third man leaned forward and looked at Clint.

Brent came along with three beers and put one in front of each man. As the three of them started to drink, they reacted as if someone had bumped into their elbows, spilling beer down the fronts of their shirts and onto the bar and the floor.

"Hey!" Carvey cried. "Goddamn it!"

"You fellas are a little clumsy, aren't you?" Clint asked.

The three of them put their beers down and stepped back, turning slightly to face Clint.

"Mister, you owe us three beers," Carvey said.

"Fine," Clint said. "Brent, give my three friends a fresh beer."

"Naw, naw," Carvey said, "you ain't gettin' off that easy. You been gettin' in our way since we got here. I think we should all step outside."

"For what?" Clint asked. "There's plenty of room in here."

"In here somebody innocent could get hurt," Dale said.

"Outside somebody innocent could get hurt, too," Clint said. "Me."

THIRTY-EIGHT

Colonel Woods spotted John Cross standing across from the large saloon tent and approached him.

"John."

Cross took his eyes off the tent for a split second, then went right back.

"Colonel."

"What's going on?"

"Clint Adams is in there," Cross said. "He has been for a while."

"Drinking?"

"I assume so."

"And you're waiting for him to come out?"

"I'm taking steps to bring him out."

"How?"

"I sent three men in after him."

"Who?"

Cross told him.

"Who are they?"

"They'll probably be my deputies," Cross said, "if they live that long."

Woods joined Cross in watching the tent.

Crapface had excellent eyesight.

The saloon tent was out of his view when he was on the ground, but from the roof he was able to see it. He was also able to see the two men—Cross and Woods—across from the tent.

He sighted down the barrel of his Sharps. It was a couple of hundred yards easily. He could see the tent, but not the entrance itself. If he was going to be helpful, they were going to have to try to kill Clint on the street.

He was starting to think he should have just followed Clint, but getting to the roof had taken a lot out of him. He didn't know if he could walk two hundred yards.

He rested the barrel of the Sharps on the edge of the roof and waited.

"Okay, then," Clint said. "Outside."

"Let's go," Gentry said.

"After my beer," Clint said. "You guys want fresh ones?"

"No," Carvey said.

"We'll be waitin' outside," Gentry said.

"I'll see you there, boys," Clint said.

The three men left.

"You really goin' out there?" Brent asked.

"I guess so."

"You could go out the back."

"And go where?"

"Three against one ain't so good odds," the bartender said.

"I've faced worse."

"Why were they pushin' you?" Brent asked.

"Some men are like that when they recognize me," Clint said.

"Helluva way to live."

"Tell me about it."

Clint finished his beer and set the empty mug down on the bar.

"See you later," he said.

"I hope so," Brent said.

Clint smiled at him, turned, and headed for the street.

When the three men exited, Woods asked Cross, "What are they doing?"

"Wait," Cross said.

Carvey looked over at Cross and nodded his head.

"They're waiting for him," Cross said. "He's coming out."

"Are you going to join them?"

"That depends on how they do," Cross said. "If they kill him, I'll take over, take the credit."

"And if he kills them?"

"Then I'll kill him," Cross said. "From here."

"That'll work," Woods said.

Crapface couldn't see what was happening right in front of the tent, but from the reactions of the two men, he assumed someone had come out. He decided to keep an eye on them until he could see someone else.

There wasn't much else he could do.

Clint stopped just in front of the tent flap. The last thing he wanted to do was kill anyone else before he left Woodsdale.

But it didn't seem like these three wanted to give him a choice.

He stepped through the flap. He saw the three men waiting, then beyond them saw Cross and the colonel.

And he understood.

THIRTY-NINE

Cross had set him up, and he was going to watch, along with the colonel.

The three men saw him come out, stiffened, then spread their feet for balance.

"About time," Carvey said.

"Is this what you fellas really want to do?" Clint asked.

"Hey," Dale said, "you were the clumsy one."

"Come on," Clint said, "we all know what this is about. Do you really want to take part in this while they just watch?"

Two of the men stared at him, but one did turn and look over at Cross and Woods before he caught himself.

Clint looked at Cross, went eye to eye with him, then looked at Woods. Both men had enough nerve to watch and catch his eye, but apparently not enough to join in.

He turned his attention back to the three men.

"Kind of silly to die over some spilled beer, don't you think?" Clint asked them.

*   *   *

Dale was the man who had turned and looked over at Cross. He wondered when the future sheriff was going to come over and back their play, like he said he would. But he quickly looked back at the Gunsmith. He wondered if the man was as good as his reputation.

"What's going on?" Woods asked.

"He's talking to them," Cross said. "He's trying to talk them out of this."

"Why?" Woods asked. "He's a gunman. Why would he talk to them?"

"Maybe he doesn't want to kill them."

"That's crazy," Woods said. "He's the Gunsmith. That's what he does. He kills people."

"Well, let's give them some time," Cross said. "It'll happen."

"Are you sure?" Woods asked. "Maybe you should go over there and help them."

"I know what I'm doing, Colonel," Cross said. "Let's just let it play out."

Carvey licked his lips, stole a glance at Gentry, who was supposed to call the play. Cross said not to worry, he'd back the play, but they should watch Gentry for the first move.

This was going to make them all big names.

Gentry swallowed. Cross had assured him that Clint Adams was past it, that he was no longer the Gunsmith his legend said he was. But the man standing in front of him looked calm, and confident.

Where was Cross? When was he going to step in?

* * *

Cross was watching the action intently. He had two plans. Gentry, Carvey, and Dale killed Adams, and he stepped in and took most of the credit. Or Adams killed them, and he killed Adams. That's how he planned it. Now it was time to see how it played, if Colonel Woods would just shut up and let it happen.

Cross put his hand on his gun.

Clint moved to his left, keeping his eyes on the three men. He found an angle where the three men were not standing between him and Cross and the colonel. But he discovered something else. From this angle he could see the porch of the hotel all the way at the end of the street. Crapface was no longer seated there. He could also see somebody on the roof of the hotel, the sun glinting off something metal.

The three men had their backs to the hotel. They couldn't see anything. The same went for John Cross and the colonel. They were so intent on the action, they weren't looking at the hotel.

Only he knew.

Crapface could see Clint now, but not whoever he was facing in the street. His best guess, though, was that it was more than one person. Since he couldn't see them, he would have to leave them to Clint. So all he could do was keep his eyes on the other two men, Cross and Woods, and wait to see if they were going to deal themselves in on the play.

FORTY

Clint decided he needed to keep his attention on the three men. He had no doubt that Crapface had somehow found out what was going on, and had gotten himself on the roof of the hotel with his Sharps. Hitting a man from there would not be an easy shot, but he could do it.

Usually.

"All right, boys," Clint said. "Time to make up your mind. Make a play, or fold."

Al Carvey and Lou Dale waited for Ed Gentry to make his move. In fact, Carvey had started to hope Gentry's move would be to walk away. He wanted to say something, but his mouth was dry. He knew they were supposed to lure the Gunsmith onto the street, but he hadn't really thought they were going to draw on him. Maybe, if he said something, Gentry would back off, and they could all walk away from this.

"Ed—" he started, but his voice seemed to put Gentry in motion.

The man went for his gun.

Gentry heard Carvey start to say something. He was so tense that, without even realizing what he was doing, he went for his gun.

He knew they were all dead.

Clint drew, shot Gentry first, since he was the first to go for his gun. The other two were grabbing at their guns in a panic, but Clint did not have the time or patience to be charitable. He didn't know what was happening across the way with Woods and Cross. He fired twice, killing Carvey and Dale before they could clear leather.

The rest was up to Crapface, two hundred yards away.

Crapface had one problem.

He figured Cross was going to be the one to go for his gun, and the colonel would watch. But the colonel was standing between him and Cross. He was going to need one of them to make a move—just a step forward or a step back would do.

Or else he'd have to fire at the colonel, and hope that his Big Fifty slug would go through and hit Cross as well.

"Damn!" Woods said. "Take him."

John Cross went for his gun. At the same moment he took a step forward, and Woods took a step back.

Woods never heard the shot, but he heard something whiz by him and strike Cross solidly. He looked at his future sheriff and saw blood spurting as the man keeled over and hit the ground.

Clint looked over at Cross and Woods, saw the would-be lawman toppling to the ground. He walked to the three bodies, checked them to make sure they were dead, at the same time replacing the spent shells in his gun with live ones. He then holstered the gun and walked toward the colonel, who looked as if he didn't know what to do, draw his gun or run. His indecision froze him in place.

"Now hold on . . ." the colonel said.

Clint looked down at Cross, then back at Colonel Woods.

"Looks like you're going to need another candidate," he said. He turned and walked away.

By the time he reached the hotel, Crapface had made his way down from the roof to the lobby. He was sitting in a chair, looking pale, and breathing hard.

"You all right?" Clint asked.

"Gimme a minute."

"That was a hell of a shot."

"Two hundred yards," Crapface said with a shrug. "Not all that hard, really. I just needed for them to move, and they did. I almost tried to take them both with the same shot."

"That would have been a hell of a shot," Clint commented.

"Yeah."

"You want to go back to your room?"

"Sure."

Clint helped Crapface get to his feet and then walked

him to the stairway. He helped him make it to the second floor.

"Are we in trouble?" he asked as they walked down the hall.

"I don't think so," Clint said. "They made it look like a fair fight, and we can claim Cross was trying to back-shoot me when you shot him. That is, if anyone even asks."

"That colonel might argue Cross was tryin' to do his job."

"Well, first he'd have to find somebody to back a new play for him," Clint said. "I told him he needs a new candidate."

"Think we should tell the fella who owns this hotel that he's got a good shot now?"

"No," Clint said. "Let him find out himself."

They got to Crapface's room and Clint opened the door. The buffalo hunter entered and sat down heavily on the bed. Getting to the roof and back had taken a lot out of him.

"How the hell did you know I was in trouble?" Clint asked.

"The girl came lookin' for you," Crapface said.

"Girl? Penny?"

"Joyce Woods," Crapface said, shaking his head. "She said she heard her father and Cross talkin' about tryin' to kill you."

"Guess I'll have to thank her."

"I think we oughtta get outta this town tomorrow, before somethin' else happens."

"Let's see how you feel in the morning," Clint said. He looked out the window. It was getting on toward dusk. He doubted the colonel would be able to put together any kind of force to come after them. At least, not before the next day.

"You get some rest," Clint said. "I'll see what's going on,

maybe get the doctor to come early in the morning to check on you."

"Good," Crapface said. "He'll give me the go-ahead to ride outta here."

Crapface sprawled out on the bed, his rifle lying right next to him.

"I'm locking the door," Clint said. "I'll knock before I come in."

"You better," Crapface said, "or I'll put a hole in ya."

As Clint stepped out into the hall and locked the door, he thought he heard his friend snoring already.

FORTY-ONE

Colonel Woods entered his house and slammed the door behind him. Joyce heard it and came running.

"What happened?" she asked. "What's wrong?"

"Adams," he said.

"Is he alive?"

"He killed three men," Woods said, "and then that friend of his killed John Cross—with a shot from the roof of the hotel."

"Oh, thank God."

Woods grabbed her by the upper arms.

"You warned them, so you got what you wanted. Now what am I supposed to do?"

"What you always do, Father," she told him, pulling away. "Think of something."

Clint came down to the lobby and, from the look the desk clerk gave him, figured word had already gotten around that he'd killed three more men. Maybe four, if he was getting credit for Cross.

He stepped outside. It was dusk, and getting darker. He decided to go back to the saloon and see what the word was. See if the bodies had been cleared from the street yet.

He stepped down from the hotel and started walking. There was no sign of Colonel Woods or anyone else on the street. The killing might have cleared the street for a few hours. Once people figured the shooting was over, they would probably come back out.

When he got to the front of the hotel, he saw that the bodies had been cleared—the three that he had left in front of the saloon, and Cross's body from across the way.

When he entered the saloon, the noise inside died down. The patrons all watched as he approached the bar.

"Well, you're back," Brent said.

"Beer," Clint said. "What's the word?"

Brent set a beer in front of him. Activity was getting back under way around them.

Brent leaned on the bar.

"Word is you gunned down those three, and then somehow managed to blow a big hole through Mr. Cross."

"I'm just amazing," Clint said.

"How did you blow a big hole through Mr. Cross?" Brent asked curiously.

"Wasn't me," Clint said. "He was killed by a Big Fifty slug."

"Ah," Brent said, "a buffalo gun—your friend?"

Clint nodded. "From the roof of the hotel."

"From that far?"

"Not too far for him," Clint said.

"Helluva shot."

"That's what I said, especially since it kept Cross from shooting me in the back."

"Looks like the colonel's gonna need a new candidate for sheriff."

"That's what I told him," Clint said. "You interested?"

"Not me. I'm happy tendin' bar."

"Anybody you know who might want the job? And I mean besides Sam Robinson?"

"Huh," Brent said, "not with you in town. Ain't nobody gonna wanna go against you after today."

"I wish that was true," Clint said.

FORTY-TWO

Think of something, Joyce had told him.

He left her and went directly to his office, closing the door behind him. All he could think of at the moment was to get Clint Adams to leave town. Then he'd have to find another candidate for sheriff. He certainly wasn't going to find another while the Gunsmith was still there. Nobody was going to want to go up against him, no matter what was at stake.

Woods hated to let Adams get away with ruining his plans. Adams and his smelly friend.

Maybe there was a way to get them taken care of after they left town? For the right amount of money somebody might agree to kill them, as long as they didn't have to face them. An ambush somewhere on the trail. Yes, that was it.

Woods knew that Sam Robinson wanted to be sheriff. With Cross gone, he'd probably win the election. But Woods figured, if he now backed Robinson, the man would be unbeatable.

So maybe he had thought of something after all.

When Clint got back to the hotel, he found Sam Robinson waiting for him in the lobby.

"Mr. Adams," Robinson said. "Is what I've been hearing true?"

"If you've been hearing that John Cross is dead, then yes, it is true."

"And you killed three other men as well?"

"That's true, too."

"Well," Robinson said, "it looks like my chances of being sheriff just improved."

"I'd say so."

"But just in case the colonel comes up with another candidate, there's still a way for me to improve my chances."

"We aren't going to talk about me running with you again, are we?" Clint asked. "Because I thought I made myself clear on that."

"Well, I just thought with the colonel trying to have you killed, you might have changed your mind."

"I haven't," Clint said, "but let me tell you what I think is going to happen."

"What's that?"

"The colonel definitely needs another candidate," Clint said, "and he might just look in one direction."

"What direction is that?"

Clint pointed at Robinson.

"You think the colonel is going to come to me?"

"Who do you think would make a better candidate?" Clint asked.

"Well . . . nobody . . . unless he comes to you."

Clint became frustrated.

"I told you, I don't want to be sheriff here, or anywhere," he said. "All I want to do is get out of here and hunt some buffalo."

"Then, this is an interesting thought," Robinson said. "The colonel coming to me?"

"Sure," Clint said, "you fellas could join forces and run this new town. Hell, this new county."

Robinson rubbed his jaw.

"I have to admit, Adams, you've given me something to think about."

"Good," Clint said, "then go and think about it. I'm tired. I'm turning in, and with any luck we'll be leaving town tomorrow."

Clint left the hotel owner standing in the middle of the lobby, still rubbing his jaw and nodding.

Upstairs Clint knocked on Crapface's door before letting himself in. Crapface was still holding the Sharps when his friend entered.

"What's goin' on?" he asked, lowering the rifle.

"I think you're right," Clint said. "Tomorrow would be a good day for us to leave. I'll get the doctor over here early and see what he says."

"Suits me."

"But no matter what he says, we'll get the hell out of here before something else happens," Clint went on. "Maybe he can bandage you up nice and tight to protect those stitches."

"I'm with you on this, Clint," Crapface said.

"Good. I'm going to turn in now. We'll be well rested when morning comes."

"Will we be alive?" Crapface asked.

"I doubt anyone will try anything tonight," Clint said. "But I'll lock your door, and mine, and I'll sleep lightly."

Clint was dozing lightly into his room when there was a knock on his door a couple of hours later. He grabbed his gun and quickly moved to the door. He turned the doorknob slowly, then yanked the door open.

"I thought we'd try it on a bed this time," Penny said.

FORTY-THREE

Actually, having Penny in bed with him the whole night turned out to be very helpful. It helped him to either stay awake or sleep lightly. As the sun came through the window, she woke with her head on his belly. She was lying on her own stomach, and when she awoke, she began to kiss him, reaching for his penis and stroking it. She kissed down his stomach until she reached his semierect cock and took it into her mouth, quickly sucking it to stiffness.

He had just been dozing, so as soon as she had awakened, he'd felt it. He put his hand on her head now as she bobbed up and down on him wetly.

She rubbed her hands on his thighs as she continued to suck him, becoming more and more eager in her oral ministrations. She moaned and hummed, working him into a frenzy, until she knew he was close to finishing, and then she withdrew and tightened her fingers around the base of his cock.

She kept him from finishing, and then began to work on

him again, licking and sucking him, until finally she climbed atop him and took him into her hot pussy.

He could have lost himself in her heat, but instead he remained aware of noises either in the hall or from across the hall, and the fact that there were none. His gun was still on the bedpost, well within his reach. But instead he reached for the girl and gave her as much of his attention as he dared, until they cried out and finished just seconds apart . . .

"I heard you were leaving today," Penny said with her head on his chest.

"Possibly," Clint said, but he was thinking it was more like definitely.

"I also heard the colonel's daughter was helpful to you."

"How do you hear all these things?" he asked.

"Hey, I work in a saloon," she said. "You hear everything there."

"I suppose you do."

"Aren't you worried she'll come up here and find us together?"

"What's the difference?" he asked. "I'm not engaged to either one of you, and I'm leaving town soon."

"When's the last time you were with a woman you loved?" she asked.

"What makes you think I don't love being with you?" he asked.

She chuckled, lifted her head, and looked at him.

"I said in love with, not love being with."

"I know you did."

"So that means you're not gonna answer the question?"

"Exactly."

She turned her head and bit him on the stomach.

* * *

Clint left Penny in his room and went to fetch the doctor. It was early, and apparently no one had gotten injured yet that day, so the doctor was available to go right back to the hotel with Clint.

They entered Crapface's room and woke the man up.

"How're you feelin'?" the doc asked.

"Good," Crapface said. "Ready to ride, right after breakfast."

"Are you hungry?"

"Starvin'," Crapface said.

"Well, that's good, then," the doctor said. "Let's have a look."

He removed Crapface's bandage, probed the wound for a few minutes, checking the stitches,

"I'll need to clean it," he said. "You did something yesterday that made you bleed a bit between the stitches."

Clint and Crapface exchanged a glance.

"I wonder what that was," Crapface said.

"Listen, Doc," Clint said, "I'm sure you heard what happened yesterday."

"I did hear something."

"Well, we have to get out of town today," Clint said. "So I think you ought to bandage that up real tight because he's going to have to ride today."

The doc sighed and said, "Well, I wouldn't recommend it, but I understand it. All right, I'll do my best."

"If you like," Clint said while the sawbones began to rebandage Crapface's shoulder, "you can join us for breakfast when we're done here."

"If you don't mind," the doctor said, "I think I'd just as soon not be around you fellas your last hour or two in town."

"Can't say I blame you for that," Clint said.

"Me, too," Crapface said.

"Good," the doctor said. "I didn't want to offend you, but—"

"No offense taken, Doc," Clint said. "I wouldn't want to be near me either when the lead starts flying."

FORTY-FOUR

When Sam Robinson heard the knock on his office door, he said, "Come in."

He wondered who'd come looking for him this early in the morning. The door opened and Colonel Woods entered the office.

"Colonel," Robinson said.

"Sam," Woods said. "We have some things to discuss."

They left the hotel and walked until they came to a tent that was serving food. The doctor said good-bye and continued on after saying, "Be careful. Colonel Woods is not a man who likes to lose."

"I'll keep that in mind," Clint said.

They sat over steak and eggs and discussed their next move.

"We're goin' right to the panhandle," Crapface said. "No more stops."

"I think we'll come to Hugoton first," Clint said.

"And we'll probably find the same thing we found here," Crapface said. "Trouble."

"You're probably right."

"I know I am," Crapface said. He shifted uncomfortably in his chair.

"You okay?"

"I'm fine," he said. "This bandage is just tight. I get on a horse I'll be fine. We stop at that other town, there's gonna be somebody there who wants to hire you, or kill you."

"I'm not arguing with you," Clint said. "I'm real happy to get away from here and let them fight over their county seat."

"You think they'll let us?" Crapface asked.

"Let us what?"

"Get away?"

"Oh yeah," Clint said. "I don't think they're going to want to deal with us anymore."

At that moment Joyce Woods came through the tent flap. She spotted them and rushed over.

"I've been looking for you," she said. "I suspected you'd be eating."

"We'll be leaving as soon as we're finished," Clint said.

"I'm leaving today, too," she said. "Going back East. I can't stay here."

"I don't blame you. What about your father?"

"Oh, he's staying," she said. "He's trying to join forces with Sam Robinson."

"I figured as much," Clint said.

She put her hand on Clint's shoulder.

"My father wants no part of you," she said. "He only wants the two of you to leave."

"Oh, we're leavin'," Crapface said. "Don't you worry about that."

She looked at him. He had his skins on again, and the smell had not improved.

He ate the last piece of steak on his late, grabbed his rifle, and said to Clint, "I'll get the horses."

"Okay."

"That big black of your ain't gonna bite off my finger, is he?"

"Be nice," Clint said. "Mention my name."

"I'll be outside."

As Crapface left, Joyce sat down. Clint waved to a waiter for the bill.

"I owe you my thanks," Clint said. "According to Crapface."

"I couldn't just stand by and watch you get killed," she said.

"I appreciate that."

"Are you really going buffalo hunting with that smelly man?" she asked.

"I am," he said. "And we're going to enjoy it."

"Why don't you come back East with me?"

"There's nothing back East for me, Joyce," he said. "My life's out here, in the West."

The waiter brought the bill and Clint paid it, then stood up. Joyce looked up at him.

"Time to go," Clint said.

"We're going in separate directions," she said. "I think I'll have a cup of tea before I go."

"Then I'll say good-bye."

"Good-bye, Clint."

Oddly, she put her hand out. He shook it, and walked out.

Outside he found Crapface standing with the horses.

"That was fast."

"I saddled yours, let somebody else saddle mine," Crap-face said, handing Clint his reins. "I wanna get out of here."

"Can you mount up on your own?" Clint asked.

"Watch me."

He struggled, but got it done. Clint mounted up.

"What did she want?"

"She wanted me to go back East with her." "Jeez," Crap-face said, "what would you do back East?"

"Exactly what I asked her," Clint said.

They wheeled their horses around and left Woodsdale, heading for the Texas panhandle and the last of the buffalo.

Watch for

THE GOVERNOR'S GUN

366th novel in the exciting GUNSMITH series
from Jove

Coming in June!

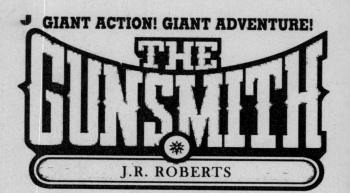

GIANT ACTION! GIANT ADVENTURE!

THE GUNSMITH

J.R. ROBERTS

penguin.com/actionwesterns

M455AS0510